THE BILLIONAIRE'S FAKE FIANCÉE

STANDALONE ENEMIES TO LOVERS ROMANCE

L. STEELE

1

Sienna

One second you think you have everything, only to lose it all the next. I lean out of the window of the penthouse of The 99, the newest condominium in Silicon Valley. Take a deep breath.

I'd gambled everything on this start-up, and failed.

The iron band around my chest tightens, and I swallow the sickness that threatens to rise.

Take the deal, Sienna.

No, I can't. To do so will go against everything I am. I'll be giving up control of my business. *My life.* Lose the very independence that made me want to become an entrepreneur.

To strike out on my own in the cut throat world of Silicon Valley where start-ups are struggling to stay alive.

"Have you decided yet?" Jace's clipped English accent scrapes the edges of my nerves.

Feet square on the ground, I turn. Those silver-green eyes slam into me with the force of a physical punch. The sparks in them glow, yet, his features stay flat.

I'm just another business transaction.

The breeze from the open window ruffles his thick hair. Over six feet tall, he towers above me.

The title of 'Angel Investor' fits Jace Walker and not only in the conventional Silicon Valley sense.

Broad shoulders clad in a crisp long-sleeved shirt. Flat stomach hinting at hidden muscles. Formal trousers mold his strong, well-shaped, thighs. Leanly built, like a runner. With those high cheek-bones and strong jaw, he could well be a fallen angel.

His eyes gleam against burnished skin in an unusual combina-tion. As surprising as the basketball hoop strung up next to his desk.

This man likes to play.

He's playing with me now. Offering me a deal he knows I must accept. If I don't, I lose everything I've built up over the last three years.

"Do you always do that?" His husky voice slides over my nerve endings.

"What?"

His eyes drop to my mouth and I redden. I'm biting my nails. A dead giveaway that I'm nervous.

Damn.

Dropping my hand to my side, I clench it into a fist.

"You'll invest a million dollars in my start-up *if* I spend a week with you?"

Unreal.

He tilts his head in agreement. Those eyes follow my every move, studying my reaction.

"It's a good deal," his voice coaxes.

One side of his lips lifts in a smile.

His charisma hits me, and I blink. This guy is lethal, with the kind of presence that'll always draw attention.

"Just small change for you." My voice is sharp with disbelief, a reminder to myself that I'm at his mercy.

After being shown the door by more than fifty potential investors, this is the first glimmer of hope I've had.

Jace Walker is one of the most eccentric investors in the Valley. He picks projects that capture his imagination, ones that don't always make financial sense at face value. I'm still surprised that he's even agreed to meet me, let alone offered to invest in my failing start-up.

And yet I can't bring myself to accept.

Why is he not offering this as a simple business loan with a high interest rate? Why attach this insane condition to it?

I have a month to pay back my debtors, or I forfeit everything. My office, my rented studio-apartment. Even my car, I remind myself. Biting the inside of my lips, I swallow down the emotions churning inside. I must stay focused. Keep my mind sharp to hold my own against this guy.

"You don't think I'm just going to hand the money over, do you? I also need some guarantee on the returns."

"The idea for my app is brilliant," I snap back. "Nothing else in the market draws up horoscopes based on people's profile pictures, then matches them to find their perfect partner."

Do our horoscopes match?

Where had that thought come from?

"An interesting premise. You just don't have enough business sense to make it a success."

I bristle, but he cuts the air with his palm in an authoritative gesture.

"If you did, you wouldn't have had to come to me."

That shuts me up.

He's right. I've let things get this far out of hand. But then, I never can do things halfway. If I believe in something, I throw caution to the wind and jump right in. I'm just not sure if I want the same in my personal life.

"Don't look so glum. A few days in London never hurt anyone. All you have to do is play the part of my girlfriend at a family wedding."

Wedding? Family? My stomach churns.

At five, an American couple had found me wandering the streets of Bombay, with no memory of my past life. My adoptive father had saved me from being run over by a car.

I'll be forever grateful to them for giving me a new life, and yet ... I still wonder about my real parents.

No, thinking about family, any family, is not my favorite pastime.

Some of my dismay must have shown, for he says, "My father has his faults, but he doesn't stint when it comes to throwing a party."

He keeps a straight face as I try to make out if he's simply leading me on with this proposal. But he seems to mean it.

"Besides, it's one of those society shindigs you women love," he adds.

"Shindigs?" I echo, struggling to keep my voice neutral.

"Yep," he nods. "The cream of London society will be there. The media will be all over it, the paparazzi trying to sneak pictures of the wedding. You'll meet some very powerful people," he adds. "With the connections you make, you could raise more funding ... even snag a rich husband."

Great, so it's not like this trip is going to stay secret; it's going to be out there for the world to see.

I'm also disappointed in Jace. I thought I'd seen intelligence in those eyes. Yet here he is, consigning me to the stereotype of a woman and what her place in the world should be. I'd been sure he was smarter than that.

And yet, something about him reaches out to me, pulls at me. I shove aside the pinpricks of awareness that dance across my skin.

I don't want to be attracted to this man.

"When your father runs Britain's largest media company, such *shindigs* must be an everyday occurrence for you," I say, my voice sharp.

His eyes narrow, and he shrugs. "No reason you can't take advantage of the opportunity when you are there."

"Don't you have a girlfriend? An ex? Someone else?" My voice is desperate in my last-ditch resort to get out of this crazy scheme.

Besides, I want to understand his intentions. Why is he suggesting such an unusual arrangement?

"You need the money. You'll do as I say, no questions asked." His voice is taut.

Ah. There it is. The smugness that comes from knowing he has me in his control. He wants to control, to manipulate. Wants someone who does as she is told.

"So what does being your girlfriend involve?"

A flash of amusement in those silver-green eyes. He takes a step forward, another. "Intimate kisses."

That pine and cloves scent of his cuts straight to my core. "Whatever it takes to convince the world that we are lovers."

He's so close now the heat leaps off his body to wrap itself around me.

"Why don't you come out and say it?" My words whisper out on a gasp. "Sex for money, is that it?"

The thought sparks a melting inside, one that confuses me.

I want this man. I may have even considered sleeping with him if he hadn't taken advantage of my helplessness, offered me this crazy deal.

"I won't do anything... not unless you ask me to." His voice is clear. Face innocent.

Yeah, right.

He runs his gaze over my body, and my nipples tighten. Dammit, he hasn't even touched me, and I'm half mad, out of my mind with wanting him.

If I give in to all his demands, I'll also give up every single shred of pride I have left.

"So, we have a deal?" His tone is cajoling, persuasive.

"No." I cut off the only means of salvaging my future.

2

____

Sienna

Silence in the penthouse. Outside a jet flies overhead, cutting through the space between us.

"Excuse me?" he grates out.

"No," I say, my voice thin yet firm. Folding my arms across my chest, nails digging into my forearms, I shake my head. "I can't do it."

A flash of pure anger ripples over his features, tightening them so his cheekbones stand out.

My heart trembles. But I will not give in. Not yet. I need the deal alright, but I must structure it to my benefit.

"If you don't take this offer, not only will you lose your start-up ... but—" he pauses for effect, "—you'll have let down your sister."

The words hang between us. My throat closes, heart thudding against my rib cage. "How did you know?" My voice comes out hoarse.

"Bella. Straight A's, brilliant student. And a gifted athlete." At his words, a trickle of sweat drips down my back.

Bella. My lovely, talented sister who'd got admission into the film-making program at UCLA, the one she's been working toward the past few years. After my adoptive father died, my mother struggled to make ends meet.

Jace is right. Without this deal I can't pay Bella's university fees. She'd have to miss the course, and that would shatter her.

I owe it to her to see this through.

I hate that Jace holds all the cards.

One day, I'll turn the tables on this man, I promise myself.

Then another thought strikes me. "You had me watched?" Even as I say it, I know it's true. "You knew I was coming today?"

"I had you researched thoroughly." He lets that sink in. "You fit the profile of the person I was looking for."

"And what is that?" I ask. Voice low. A slow burn of annoyance in the pit of my stomach.

"Attractive, intelligent, with a thirst for new experiences. Open enough to not be scared from the unusual. Yet also desperate to make it in the Valley at any cost."

Desperate enough to take his deal.

Hearing myself slotted so neatly into a pigeon-hole strikes at the very core of who I am: someone who refuses to be pegged. I will not be restrained.

He's right, though. I have a weakness for new experiences. Ask me to try something for a first time, and I can never say no. I decide right then I'm going to surprise him, shock him out of his 'billionaire' comfort zone.

He had the proposal lined up even before meeting me. Confident that I'd accept the deal. It didn't have anything to do with him wanting to invest in my start-up.

This has been about him all along. Him needing someone he could control. Anger flares to life, a bitter taste in my mouth.

I lean over and slap him.

Gold ignites in those silver-green eyes.

Silence. I'm not sorry I slapped him. Yet, the sensible part of me insists this is not going to help me at all.

A strange expression on his face, *grudging respect.*

"I deserved that," he drawls. Lips quirk in a self-deprecating smile. *A first genuine smile.*

It throws me. Makes me wary. This man is potent, disarming when he turns on the charm.

"I'm sorry," I lie.

"Your temper's going to make things a lot more *interesting* in the next few days," he growls, voice predatory.

No missing the unmistakable sexual meaning of his words.

A sharp curl of desire twists my stomach.

"I mean no harm." He holds up his hands.

A gesture meant to placate.

I trust him as much as a wild jaguar.

"Agree to the deal, and I'll ensure the first installment of half a million hits your account before the end of the day. More than enough to pay off your urgent business debts. And your sister's fees."

Bella had been born five years after my parents adopted me. My baby sister is the light of my life.

Oh. He knows exactly what to say to get me to agree. I resent being manipulated this way, and yet ... what choice do I have?

I know when I've been out maneuvered. But at least Bella will be fine and so will my team, for now.

Holding onto that thought, I jerk my head. "I'll do it," I say, voice cold. Even as my heart stutters in nervousness.

He tilts his head, acknowledging my response. *Did a flicker of relief cross his features?*

He needs me to do this more than he's letting on.

"On one condition," I add.

His jaw hardens.

"Separate bedrooms," I burst out before I lose my nerve.

He snaps back, "Same suite. Same bed. We must keep the pretense up behind closed doors too. We'll be at a hotel and staff talk. We have to ensure no word of this arrangement gets out, not even a whiff."

His voice is authoritative, brooks no argument. *End of discussion.*

I blink.

How dare he command me?

If he paid for my time, I'll have to do as he says, no questions asked, over the next week.

That part of me that hates being constrained resists. No. I can't let him have so much power over me.

And yet, that hidden, treacherous part of me so attracted to him leaps to life. The thought of sleeping in the same bed as him... How would it feel to have those fingers on my skin? Sliding down the curve of my waist, toward the dip of my—

Don't go there.

"My lawyer will swing by your place this evening with the agreement, including a non-disclosure clause." He keeps his voice casual but I sense the underlying tension.

Yeah, he wants this formalized before I change my mind. Makes me wonder why he's so desperate to have a girlfriend accompany him on this trip. *I'm going to find out.*

"No part of this conversation is to be mentioned to anyone. Not your close friends or family or even ex-boyfriends." Emphasis on the last word sets my teeth on edge. "And no speaking to the press, of course."

"Yeah, I get it. I'm not stupid," I mutter, anger crawling up my spine. I hate feeling so helpless.

"No, you're not." He holds out his hand.

I don't take it. Don't even respond to the gesture.

No change of expression in his face. He only cares that I've accepted his proposal. My feelings don't come into this equation.

"We leave in two days." His voice is matter of fact.

"So soon?" I squeak.

"Yeah." He runs his fingers through his hair. "We fly out, spend a couple of days with the family. The wedding is on Sunday night."

I almost choke. An entire week in close quarters with this man? Seven days of pretending I'm in love with him, can't live without him...even as I resist this strange pull I feel toward him.

Hell.

Unaware of the emotions churning inside, he continues, "You also can't bring your personal phone or your laptop or be in touch with anyone these next few days."

"What?"

He's mad.

"To avoid any temptation of photos, emails, telling anyone else where you are or what you're up to," he says. "We need to keep media attention out of this completely."

"You're cutting me off from the world? Don't trust me?" I'm only half kidding.

His reaction doesn't disappoint.

Silver sparks flare. "I never underestimate my opponent."

He has no idea what I'm capable of.

"Besides, it's only for a few days, and I'm making it worth your while, aren't I?"

Yeah, and *I'm* paying a big enough price for it. But I don't say that aloud.

In a daze, I turn toward the door, making to leave when his voice calls out, "You'll need the right clothes, won't you? I'll arrange for a credit card."

Right. Credit card. I half turn, sure this time I look plain baffled.

"You'll be fine, Sienna," he says in a gruff voice.

The sound of my name on his lips feels strangely intimate.

What have I gotten myself into?

3

Jace

Later that evening

"Fuck." Jace swears as the barbell almost slips from his hands. His muscles are tired after an hour of intense exercise. Yet, the workout session has not cleared his mind. Gleaming amber eyes haunt him, along with images of lush auburn hair rippling down her back, making him want to curl the thick strands around his palm.

The photographs the PI had shown Jace had not done Sienna justice.

For one thing, they hadn't hinted at that black coffee and vanilla scent of her. Or that curvy waist, or the hips that flared so seductively that his attention had gone right there and stayed. Part angry, part innocent, she was all liquid fire. An intense urge to lean in and taste the skin at the hollow of her neck had gripped him. The force of his desire taking him by surprise.

And when his eyes had traveled back to her face, he'd found her cheeks flushed. The rapid rise and fall of her chest showing that he'd been affecting her, too.

The force of the attraction was so strong; he'd almost withdrawn his proposition. If he spent time with her, he'd end up sleeping with her. It's inevitable. Perhaps that's all it is. Lust. *He must take her to bed and get it over with.* Jace plans to do that at the first possible opportunity.

His mind made up, Jace places the barbell with the weights back on the rack, and then sits up.

Reaching for the towel, he wipes away the sweat running down his forehead. As he glugs down water from his bottle, his eyes take in the men around him in the small, sweaty gym not far from The 99.

A few blocks away from his penthouse and it's a different reality. A slightly rundown area of the city. Jace had specifically chosen this gym for its no-frills feel. An honest-to-goodness workout space, with a boxing ring at the center where two of his friends are going a few rounds. He winces when Eric gets in a punch at Damian.

Damian's upper body snaps back from the force of the blow. He springs right back, holding up his fists to guard his face. Damian takes the hammering, but Jace knows it's unwise to underestimate him. Damian's as mean in the ring as on stage, able to hold his own against his fighting opponent as ably as he holds the attention of crowds at his concert.

"Ouch, that must hurt."

Jace looks up as his friend Arpad walks up to him, wearing a cut off T-shirt with blotches of sweat on the chest.

"Nice color," Jace smirks. "Brings out the blue of your eyes."

"Oh." Arpad looks down at the light blue of his shirt. "One of my team-members may have gifted it to me."

"Do they always do that? Give you little tokens in the hope of winning your affection?"

Arpad's name had recently appeared on the top 40-under-40 list of bankers in the country. He's no less famous than Damian in his own field.

"Girls," Arpad cuts the air with the underside of his palm. The gesture's elegant, and would have looked feminine coming from anyone else. From Arpad it seems eloquent, and as European as the country he comes from.

"Those two don't like each other, do they?" asks a husky voice as Karina swaggers over to join them.

She wears stretch pants and a low cut sports-bra that shows off her sculpted abs. The sweat on her forehead makes her skin glow.

"Au contraire." Arpad grins. "Eric and Damian are best buddies. Trust each other enough to go at it whenever they meet in the ring. Eric and Jace here have more fights as business partners and ones far more vicious than what you see there."

Jace stiffens at the description of his and Eric's business relationship. It's true they often have differing points of view on how to expand the business. That's also the reason Jace had taken Eric on as his business partner, hoping their opinions would balance each other out.

Now Jace wonders if he had miscalculated. Perhaps he and Eric are too different to work together.

"Men!" Karina snorts. Her almond shaped eyes narrowed at the edges, lending an air of exotica to her face.

"But what would you do without us, darling?" Arpad slips his arm around Karina, in a 'we are just friends' fashion, only to have her raise an eyebrow at him.

"Your banker-wanker charms don't work on me." Her voice is casual. *Too casual.*

"Careful, Arpad," Jace chuckles. "She's the most lethal of all of us and you know that."

It's true, Jace realizes, even as he says it. Karina had trained with her father in the martial arts since she was five. At eighteen, she'd started her own security business. Now she provided bodyguards for some of the biggest names in Hollywood and in the corporate world.

"Hey." Arpad rubs the place over his heart, in mock pain, widening his eyes, "I wasn't flirting, honest."

"Yeah." Karina snorts again. "You can't help but pounce on anything in a skirt. At least Jace here is more discerning."

"Am I?" Jace asks, surprised.

Is that why he's never been in a long-term relationship even though he's almost thirty? All the more reason Jace's reaction to Sienna is so surprising. The intensity of the attraction has shaken him more than he'll care to admit.

"Hey, you." Jace starts as Karina ruffles his hair, her gesture affectionate. "Where did you go to?"

"Not fair," Arpad protests. "He gets his hair fluffed, and I don't even get a hello."

"You, Mr. Money Bags, are an out-and-out shark. You should be grateful that, despite being a banker, you still have friends," Karina replies.

"Ouch." Jace laughs aloud as he gets to his feet.

"You don't laugh." She turns on him. "You, Mr. Angel Investor like control too much. You think you can control your destiny and the people in your life, you think wrong. You never know when fate has a surprise right around the corner."

Jace blinks, puts up his hands in a gesture of surrender. "You're right, of course."

"Ha," Karina snorts. "You charmer, you."

Sliding an arm around Karina, Jace slaps Arpad on the back. "We men have to stick together sometimes too." Jace tells Arpad. "We're here for you, you know that."

When Karina speaks next, her tone is serious, "In this town where only money speaks, here in this gym, we're all equal. It's why we hang out here, right?"

Jace nods, his features solemn, remembering how they'd met. A few years ago, it had been only the five of them working out late one night at this gym.

A loud argument from the gym-manager's office had attracted Arpad and Jace.

Turned out Bosco, who ran the gym, didn't have money to meet his rent. His landlord had arrived with his team, threatened to evict him.

On the spot, Arpad had offered to pay off his dues.

But even that had no effect. The landlord wanted Bosco out so he could sell up to a developer.

Things had gotten ugly when the landlord's man attacked the two of them. Eric, Damian and Karina had helped fight the thugs off.

The five had pooled in money, helped Bosco buy the gym outright, making them all part-owners.

Now they hung out here, a close friendship having sprung up between them.

Karina's right. In this gym, it doesn't matter who they are, or how much money they have. Here it's about working out. Honest sweat that strips each of them of the veneer they often have to present to the world.

In the boxing ring, Eric throws a final punch and Damian hits the floor with a thud. Stays still.

Too still.

Eric strips off his gloves and his head guard, dropping down to check on his friend.

At the same time, Karina breaks out in a run toward the ring, followed closely by Jace.

Ahead, Arpad has already reached the ring, leaping up. He and Eric turn Damian over.

Silence.

"Fuck, is he okay?" Eric asks, worry lacing his voice.

"Dammit, he's bleeding," Karina snarls.

The worry in her voice pushes Jace to clamber up into the raised platform of the ring, hauling Karina up after him. By that time Damian's shoulders are shaking.

"What the fuck—?" Jace exclaims, wondering if Damian is going into cardiac arrest.

Eyes springing open, Damian sits up. "Just checking what you guys would have done if I'd actually been really hurt." He grins, the lazy Texas drawl evident in his laughing voice.

"What the—"

"Bastard."

Eric and Arpad leap on Damian, the three going down in a tangle of arms and legs. Jace folds his hands over his chest, his gaze meeting Karina's in a shared look of amusement. She raises her eyebrows, taps her finger to her forehead, an indication of exactly how ridiculous she thought the men on the ground were.

Skirting the men still play-fighting, she walks over to Jace. "How is the start-up investment business these days?" She asks.

Jace stays silent, his expression non-committal. While he's close to all four of the group, Karina and he had bonded almost instantly. She regards him as a sibling, a younger brother. She's the only one of the group to whom he's hinted a little about his financial setbacks.

"Have you and Eric agreed to a plan on what to do next?" Karina asks.

4

Jace

Jace looks to the boxing-ring in the little gym. To where Eric is sprawled on the floor. His body almost hidden under the combined bulk of Arpad and a still-bleeding Damian. All three are locked in a tangle of arms and legs.

"No, I haven't mentioned my plan to Eric yet," he finally replies to Karina's question.

Guilt threads through Jace.

As his business partner, Eric deserves to know the plan he's put into place to rescue their business.

Jace comes from one of the most moneyed families in the UK, a fact he neither hides nor flaunts.

Unlike Eric, who came from a humble background, his father an immigrant from Mexico. But that only makes Eric more determined to succeed.

Jace had made a series of risky investments in the past year. Eric had protested each decision, but given in at Jace's vehement belief that they would succeed.

After all, Jace had a track record of being able to pull off long shots. Besides, Jace had invested his money in the business. Eric had invested his time. And Jace had paid him for it. Technically that made Eric his employee, but they'd always functioned as business partners.

Eric was right, though. This time he'd overstretched. Not one of the start-ups had broken even.

Now they stand to lose all they had invested.

It's Jace's fault they're in this mess.

And Jace is determined to put it right.

As the scion of the Walker empire, Jace's father owned a huge chunk of media interests around the world. And now Jace must get the first installment of his inheritance from his father, and invest it in the business. It's the only way to save his and Eric's future—whether Eric agrees with his approach or not.

"Things are bound to get ugly before they get better. Besides, I have a plan." Jace's grin is cocky. Too quick.

"Hmm." Karina's eyes snap onto his and hold, a worried look in hers.

"You'll tell me if you need money? We'd all help, you know that?" she says.

At that, Jace drops the uncaring look he's been trying so hard to feign. His heart melts a little. He's unused to having a circle of friends to fall back on. He'd grown up isolated, first in his father's country mansion near London, then at boarding school.

No, he hadn't expected to forge such strong friendships in this little gym in a seedy part of one of the most commercially minded cities in the world.

Leaning down, he brushes Karina's cheek with his lips. An affectionate kiss.

Before he can say anything further, Eric's on his feet. He limps over to them. Sweat drips down his forehead. His shorts are dirty, his T-shirt torn from the fight.

"Leg bothering you?" Jace asks before he can stop himself.

"No more than usual." Eric's reply is short.

Jace knows Eric hates being reminded of his impediment. Growing up in the slums of Mexico City had resulted in Eric being in a gang fight that left him with a permanent limp. His family had been unable to afford the medical care required to heal him then.

His parents had migrated to the US when Eric was ten. It's been a hard climb up for Eric to get to where he is now, Jace knows that.

But his physical impairment has only left Eric with an iron-willed work ethic and a need to excel at anything he takes up, including feats of physical prowess. Eric now trains for marathons, determined to show that not even his slight physical disability can stop him. His single-mindedness is much the same when it comes to succeeding at business.

It's what makes Eric a valuable business partner.

"You look like you've been in a cat-fight," Karina tells Eric in a tone that drips ice—a tone that's subdued many a celebrity into following her orders.

Just then Damian stalks toward their group. His gait—one that tends to drive the women at his rock concerts wild with lust—is familiar to fans around the world. "Good fight." Damian slaps Eric on the back.

The two clasp hands.

"Sorry about that pretty face," Eric needles the other guy.

"You don't look so good yourself, hotshot," Damian shoots right back.

"You two are in better shape than him." Karina points to Arpad still sprawled in the center of the ring. "And he didn't even fight."

Walking to Arpad, Jace hauls the banker to his feet. "Come on, moneybags. To the showers."

"We're going to the bar. You coming?" Arpad calls out to Karina as they jump down from the ring.

"You mean your favorite dive bar, up the block?" Karina asks.

At Arpad's nod, Karina shudders. "Not a chance," she exclaims. "Wild animals can't drag me in there."

"Can wild men?" Arpad calls out.

"You're looking at the wrong person to kiss your wounds better," Karina smirks. "Besides, I have a date to head to."

She jumps down from the ring on the other side, flounces off toward the female changing room, to whistles from the men.

"Who's the lucky guy?" Arpad snaps, his tone angry.

But Karina doesn't notice. "None of you, that's for sure." She grins. Pausing at the entrance to the changing room, she waves. "Don't wait for me. I'm heading home first to get pretty." Her smile is wicked.

Arpad makes as if to follow her, his face twisting with emotion. He's jealous of Karina's date. Jace holds Arpad back, shakes his head. "You go after Karina now, you lose her forever."

"So I stand by and watch as she fucks half the men in this town?" Arpad snarls, but beneath that anger, pain is evident.

Jace grips his friend's shoulder. "Sometimes you have to explore what's outside to recognize what you have right in front of you."

Right. He's giving Arpad advice on how to handle his love life, when Jace's own is about to get more complicated than it's ever been.

Eric calls out to them from the entrance of the changing room, "You guys coming or do you want to spend all evening gossiping like old ladies?"

That breaks the somber mood of their conversation. Arpad pulls out of Jace's grasp to follow Eric into the changing room.

Half an hour later Eric and Jace are seated at a small table at the far corner of the 'dive bar' that Karina so hates. It's more rundown than the gym, and filled with the kind of people Jace would never meet on a daily basis.

Sheer proximity to the gym had the four men veering toward the bar the same night they had met—the only time so far that Karina had accompanied them. Heading here once a week had become a habit.

They had an unspoken agreement to leave the high profile of their daily lives behind on these evenings.

It's a cover of sorts, Jace supposed. In here, they didn't have to pretend. They could just be a group of friends catching up on each other's lives.

The smack of a pool ball cuts through his thoughts, and Jace knows he can't put off talking to Eric any longer.

Chugging down a healthy swallow of the whiskey, Eric grimaces. "What is this?"

Jace barks out a laugh. "Laphroaig. Jerry keeps a bottle behind the bar, only for us."

Eric's eyes dart to the bartender, "Ah. One for the big billionaire boys who grace his establishment, is it?"

A hint of the bitterness slips through, giving away that Eric is very aware that he doesn't belong to that club. Yet.

Jace wants to protest that Eric is putting himself down too much.

Eric may not have Damian's talent, or Jace's moneyed background or even Arpad's choice of profession that had catapulted him onto the rich list very quickly. But he has grit and determination in plenty.

Sure, Jace grew up the son of a media magnate, but Darren, his father, was self-made. He'd never allowed his only son to forget that. It's why Jace is here in Silicon Valley, trying to make it on his own. Darren owns a clutch of newspapers and TV channels, but has no interest in breaking into Silicon Valley. Jace wants it to stay that way.

"I'm going to London to get the first installment of my inheritance," Jace says. "I'll put it right back into the business."

Eric's eyes widen, "Thought you weren't on speaking terms with your father? Besides, aren't there conditions attached to getting the first installment?"

"Yeah." Jace's fingers tighten around his glass. "The old man's gone senile. He wants me to show I'm serious about settling down and producing an heir before he releases it."

"And how are you going to convince him? The last I knew, you were single. Unless you've managed to grow a girlfriend in the last twenty-four hours?"

Jace chuckles.

Eric's forehead crinkles in a frown, "You didn't."

When he stays silent, Eric exclaims, "You convinced a woman to come to London with you?"

Jace nods. "It's Natalie's wedding in a week's time in London. I'm going, 'adoring' girlfriend in tow."

"How did you find this 'girlfriend'?" Eric's voice is suspicious.

Jace takes another swig of the whiskey. "Amazing what a million dollars will get you."

Eric chokes over his own drink. Reaching for the bottle of water, he drinks half of it before speaking. "A million dollars to spend a week with you?"

Jace nods.

"Your methods are unorthodox, to say the least. I love you like a brother, have always stood by your choices, but this time you've gone too far." Eric's voice has an edge to it.

It's Jace's turn to frown. His eyebrows slash down over his nose.

"It didn't cross your mind that what you are doing is bizarre?" Eric asks. "Manipulating someone into accompanying you, and then agreeing to give her a million dollars? That wipes out the remaining funds in the business. Not to mention that the ethics of it are highly questionable."

Jace's muscles tense. A part of him agrees with Eric's rationale. In fact, put like that, it sounds a bit crazy, even to him.

"I didn't manipulate Sienna." Jace insists. "I made a business proposition, and she accepted. Besides, the million will pay for itself manifold. Just the first installment of my inheritance runs to five billion."

Eric whistles. "Serious money. I can see why you're trying to pull off this crazy stunt. Of course it all depends on your gamble paying off. If it does."

"*When* it pays off," Jace insists with more confidence than he actually feels.

He'd gone with his gut, made the offer to Sienna. Jace had staked their last million on this play. He'd know soon whether it'd work or not. The last thing he wants to do is discuss the ethics of his actions.

"Let me do this my way. Give me a chance to bail us out of this mess," he says, voice uncompromising.

"That's what you said the last time." Eric's voice is wry; his face wears a half-smile.

"And I pulled through then," Jace reminds his business partner.

Eric steeples his fingers over the whiskey glass. "Careful, Jace." His voice is serious. "You're treading a thin line. You never know when your next play may be your last."

And *that*'s the biggest difference between the two of them.

No matter what the challenge, Jace has an innate confidence that he'll overcome it. Perhaps it was blind faith born of always having a safety net, a back-up in his Dad's money, as Eric often remarked. But Jace knows it's more than that. He has an inherent belief in himself and in the idea that things meant to come to him would ultimately find their way.

And those things that didn't come to him? Well, they simply weren't meant to be.

Unlike Eric, who had a knack of underestimating himself. He preferred to believe in the worst possible outcome.

Eric called it being 'realistic.' A mindset that often stopped him from taking risks.

One Jace doesn't subscribe to.

Damian and Arpad arrive with their drinks, interrupting Jace's train of thought and sliding into their cramped booth.

The four clink glasses.

"What are we toasting?" Damian asks.

"To London." Eric is the first to go, voice sardonic.

"Who's going to London?" Arpad demands.

"Jace is, for a business transaction. Which means as his business partner, I am, too, to ensure he stays out of trouble," Eric replies, humor in his voice.

Jace inclines his head, accepts the criticism.

"And you, Arpad, what are you toasting to?" Jace asks.

"To sassy women who get under my skin," Arpad says, voice wry.

"Do they also happen to head up their own security companies?"
Damian grins.

Arpad makes a gun with his fingers, mimes shooting him.

"And you, Damian?" Eric asks.

"To sex, women and rock shows. May the ride continue."

Jace is the last to raise a toast. He hesitates, choosing his words
with care.

"To rolling the dice, one last time."

Eric chuckles. "Good luck, amigo."

As they clink glasses, Jace wonders why, despite his best intentions, he can't get rid of this sinking feeling that he's going to lose this
time.

5

Sienna

Two days later

When my alarm goes off, I sit up with a start. My first thought is that I am going to see *him* today.

Silver-green eyes. Sardonic voice. The strength in those shoulders. Merely thinking of him sends a curl of heat rising in my belly.

And I plan to spend an entire week with him?

I swear aloud. I'll never be able to resist him.

Is it too late to call it all off?

As if in answer, an email pings in my inbox. Reading the subject, I wince. It's from the landlord, reminding me I owe him last month's rent on the office.

And then there's Bella.

It'd been stupid of me to think I could manage it all. If only I could turn the clock back. Back to before I'd left home. Before my adoptive father died in an accident and I'd sworn to take care of my sister.

My throat tightens. I'm well and truly trapped.

Conceding defeat is not an option. Not unless I have exhausted every single possibility of being funded. And strange as this offer is, it still means securing the money.

It's this or becoming homeless. Perhaps I should have considered that waitressing job at the corner coffee shop? Even as I think of it, I abandon that idea. *Not practical.*

But spending a week with a strange Angel Investor is?

Besides, I've committed already. I must go through with it. And hope I can resist him. Resist that powerful pull to him that has me in thrall.

Bracing myself, I place my feet on the floor. A gentle hammering starts in my head and I groan aloud, cursing the cheap wine from last night. *That's all I need now, a hangover.*

By the time I finish a quick shower and am on my second cup of coffee, I feel almost human. The intercom buzzes.

I'm not ready to face my future, yet here it is.

Wheeling my suitcase out of the building, I barely register the chauffeur who springs to attention and takes it from me. I slide into the back seat, but Jace doesn't even look up or acknowledge me. He continues staring at his tablet.

Annoyed at being ignored, I look out of the window as the limo pulls away. Still, my eyes find their way back to him. Faded jeans, tan loafers. A leather jacket hangs on the peg next to him.

He's wearing a T-shirt, short sleeves reveal the beginnings of a tattoo on his right bicep.

Tattoo?

It only adds to his reputation of being eccentric, hints at a misspent youth. Curious, I follow the design, which sweeps up, disappearing inside the sleeve only to reappear, peeking above the neckline.

A strange intricate design, letters in a language that I vaguely recognize.

It's Hindi.

A language I'd heard growing up in Bombay. Faint images of those years often come back.

A woman's laughter.

Tinkling of anklets.

Echoes of voices. Words I don't understand, but often I feel their underlying emotions.

I blink and shake my head to clear it, and when I take a breath to calm myself, the smell of sea air, fresh, tangy flows over me. Desire unfurls in the pit of my stomach.

Before I can question why he has a tattoo in the language of my birth country, he says, "Good morning."

His voice slides over my skin, sinking in. It accelerates the slow burn inside, and all other thoughts go out of my head.

Ridiculous, this reaction to him.

I grunt, not trusting myself to speak. Instead, close my eyes behind my sunglasses and lean back against the seat.

"Hungover, are we?" His tone is mild, humor lurking beneath the words.

The patronizing 'we' in his sentence grates on my nerves. I'm about to retort, but he's already turned back to his tablet, frowning at it.

Spying the stock market reports up on his screen, I say, "Busy, *are we*?" I try to mirror the same degree of boredom I heard in his voice.

Fail.

I just come across as interested in what he's doing.

He replies without looking up from the screen, "We have an IPO coming out—" He stops mid-sentence, as if losing track of his thoughts. Opening up a fresh window on his tablet, he composes an email. I don't want to snoop but can't take my eyes of his fingers flying over the keyboard.

Long, tapered fingers.

Sensitive fingers.

How would they feel on my skin?

A little shiver runs down my back.

Firing off the email, he sets aside the tablet. His eyes sweep over me. I'd pulled on my oldest T-shirt in defiance. Refusing to dress up for him. A last stance at rebelling.

Stupid.

The T-shirt is comfortable. Also threadbare. When his eyes alight on my breast, my nipples harden. I'm sure they are outlined against the thin material.

I'd made sure I'd shopped using his credit card. A lot. Yet, by the end of my little expedition, I was nowhere near maxing out the credit card. So, I'd called the bank to ask for the limit. The amount had made my mouth go dry. I could have shopped all year and still not hit *that* number. Even thinking about the kind of money this man is made of makes my head spin. It also makes me wary. Men with such money are used to buying, owning. Possessing. *Like he owns me now for the next few days.*

The sunlight pours through the window, draping his shoulders, picking out hints of silver in those silver-green eyes. I take in the breadth of his shoulders, the shirt stretching across his chest and down over his stomach—which would be flat. Hard.

Desire pools in my chest, making it difficult to breathe.

"Like what you see?" he drawls.

"Do you?" I snap back.

His eyes light up with a strange gleam, and he looks over me again. This time deliberately lingering on my lips, the swell of my breasts, and then pointedly at the apex of my thighs.

His gaze sweeps down my jean clad legs before coming back up to rest on my face.

A dense pulse of heat from him reaches out to me.

He's aroused. And by the time he's done checking me out, I am too. That slow burn in my belly throbs.

He hadn't been gentle when he looked this time.

He won't be a gentle lover. The thought comes unbidden to my mind. I bite my lips, stay silent.

He pauses, wringing out the silence, stretching my nerves before replying, "Very much."

His voice is serious, no trace of humor in it.

He wants me.

Wants to take me right now, right here.

The blood rushes to my cheeks. The space between us seems to shrink, and I have this sudden urge to reach out and touch him.

"Stop it."

"What?" His voice is innocent.

"This." I point to the space between us. "Stop turning on that charm, trying to seduce me with your eyes."

He laughs, sounding startled. "Does it make you uncomfortable?"

There's a hint of curiosity and something almost animalistic in his voice. As if he's found a weakness and will not hesitate to use it against me.

I shrink back a little from him and try to pull my thoughts together. He reads me too easily. I must learn to hide my emotions better.

"What do *you* think?" I ask, my voice neutral.

"I think you have a vivid imagination." The edge of his lips lift in a half-smile. He takes my hand, holding it for a second longer than necessary.

The warmth from his fingers seeps into my skin, flowing through my blood. My cheeks go warm. Pulse racing, I tug away from his hand and he lets go.

Looking at the screen of his tablet, he touches it, then hands it to me. "There, the money's in your account," he says.

Sure enough, the transfer has gone through. Half a million dollars. The most money I have seen in my life.

My gut churns. I hand the tablet over to him, swallowing down the bile that threatens to rise.

Bella is going to be fine. And I should have enough to see off the worst of the creditors. Jace has bought me a month at least.

I'm about to mutter a thank you when he says, "I have one condition."

His voice is deceptively quiet. Too quiet.

"What?" I growl.

"Regardless of what you see and hear over the next few days, you'll fulfill your end of the bargain. You'll stay with me, see this one through to the end."

I bite my lips.

That's what he asked for already, isn't it? Except this time there is an urgency to his voice, as if this is important to him. So important perhaps his future depends on it, too.

Even as the thought strikes me, I almost reel from the intensity in those silver-green eyes. They burn with a fierceness I haven't seen before.

I nod, wordless.

For the first time, I realize the seriousness, the sheer stupidity, of the situation.

I can't back out now.

No doubt Jace will stick to his word, and not force me to sleep with him. The question is, can I resist the temptation to seduce him?

6

Sienna

"Sienna?"

The soft smell of the pine and cloves wafts over me. I lean into it.

The voice calls again. This time there's a touch of humor in it, which cuts through the layers of sluggish sleep.

I come awake in an instant, to find him watching me.

The green in his eyes swirl, drawing me in. He leans in to touch my cheek and a shudder runs through me, breaking the spell.

"Jace?" My voice comes out rough.

I clear my throat to dispel the remnants of sleep.

He doesn't reply. His breath ruffles my hair, shuddering over my skin.

I want to touch his hair, his lips. Run my hands over the skin of his neck.

His eyes dilate into pinpricks of green. Then he's moving back and out of the car.

I blink, look out the window. We're parked on a runway. I've slept through the short ride.

Heaving my bag over my shoulder, I follow Jace to the small plane, gleaming silver in the sunlight. Up a small flight of steps into the door. When I walk in, my feet sink into the carpet, muffling the sound from my sneakers.

"Hello."

I look up in surprise at the man who appeared in front of me.

"Didn't mean to startle you," he says.

He's a comfortable height so I can look at him without having to crane my neck. Brown hair tops his pleasant face crinkled in a wide smile.

"I'm Eric."

At the question on my face he chuckles. A friendly sound. One that warms my heart and makes me trust him immediately.

"Guess Jace neglected to tell you I was coming along." His exasperated tone makes me smile.

The tension in my shoulders dissipates. "You're coming to London with us?"

Eric nods. "Bet you're relieved not to be on your own with *that*." He points toward Jace now seated at the back of the small plane, head bent over his tablet already.

"You have no idea." I lower my voice to match his.

"Don't worry, I'll protect you from the evil beast." His mock-serious words prompt a nervous giggle from me.

Jace looks at us, and then stares at Eric, who stiffens.

Something passes between them. A light touch on my shoulder as Eric guides me to one of the comfortable twin seats opposite Jace.

Eric takes the seat behind me.

As the door to the plane slams shut, I cringe. *This is it.*

When the plane begins to taxi, I feel as if I'm leaving behind everything familiar. Comfortable. *Boring.*

I'm shedding the girl from small town Gainesville who had come to Silicon Valley chasing a dream.

Now I am a woman of the world, en route to London, with a boyfriend who loves her.

Except that's not true either.

Truth is, I'm going to a city halfway around the world, with a man I barely knew. And who's going to expect sexual favors of me.

What does that make me?

A fake girlfriend?

A call girl for hire?

No. Just someone desperate to do right by her family and her employees. Someone who had bet it all on an idea and lost. I'd been so confident that I could make it happen. I had never even given thought to what would happen if it all went wrong.

Optimist that I was. Or plain foolish, really. And now I must pay the price. My stomach rolls a little as the flight takes off and I grip my seat, to stave off the sickness rising to my throat.

"Cold feet?"

Jace is perceptive all right. He'd had to be to make it this far in the business world.

"If it's any consolation, I haven't done anything like this before." He sounds a little taken aback himself.

I want to trust the authenticity of his words.

No way. He's a master manipulator, is all. He's trying to win me over, relax the tension between us so our relationship feels more genuine to his family.

"No," I snap, "just realizing this is how the other half lives."

"You mean the plane?" He looks around him. "Merely trappings."

He raises his shoulders and the movement stretches his T-shirt across his chest.

My eyes are at once drawn to the tattoo that peeks out above the neckline. I resist the urge to follow the shape of the corded neck muscles toward his chin. Instead, I stare out the window as we continue to climb, tearing through the clouds.

"It's okay to look." Sliding the tablet into the sleeve set against the wall, he reaches toward me.

I shrink back.

He leans close, and my breath catches in my throat.

Fresh pine, and sweet cloves. He smells wild and earthy. Sensual. I can see the creases at the edges of his eyes. That full lower lip that hints at hidden depths, invites me to sink my teeth into it.

And before I can stop myself, I lean forward to do exactly that. When he snaps my seatbelt into place with a resounding click, I jump, blinking in surprise.

Jace leans back, eyes gleaming.

Oh. He enjoyed that little trick.

My nails bite into my palm. I will not slap him again. Will not.

The sun's rays slant through the window, blinding me for a second. Then the plane breaks through the clouds, and levels out. Now we glide, the difference startling after the bumpy ride of the few seconds ago.

"Your first trip to London, right?" He asks.

"You went to boarding school in England, didn't you?" I respond.

Question for question. Only fair.

That gets his attention.

"Did some research of my own." I pause. "Google search."

His features relax.

"Do you miss London at all?"

He glances out the window before replying, his voice short. "No."

I wince at the bite in his tone.

A shutter comes down over his features.

"Sorry," he says, in a calmer tone, sounding very English right then. "I don't miss the people there. But I do miss the way of life. There is a kind of grace, a love for the softer aspects of life in London."

"An angel investor who also sounds poetic?" I exclaim.

I hadn't expected him to say something that hints at the man behind the persona—the ambitious businessman trying to break out of his father's shadow.

That much I'd read between the lines of his interviews online.

He chuckles, a full, deep-throated sound that rumbles up from his chest.

His features relax, making him look younger.

So far, he's been aloof, shut off, only the occasional flash of intelligence hinting at the sharp brain behind that lazy charm. But relaxed like this, he's more open. And it's as if I can feel him for the first time.

Strictly business, remember?

This is a business trip.

Right.

"So what's the story?" I ask.

"Story?" He asks, eyebrows slashing down.

"Us," I point from me to him. "How did we meet? Any deep dark secrets about your past I should know?" I bat my eyelashes. "After all, if we're lovers"—I gulp as the word sends a spurt of melting heat through me—"then we must have exchanged *some* intimacies?"

"Intimacies," Jace drawls out the word. A promise of all kinds of naughty, pleasurable things.

Not good.

"Love at first sight," I snap before he can say anything else.

"What?" Jace frowns.

"You saw me across a crowded room, at a cocktail party. Fell in love with me." I say.

Jace continues the story without blinking. "And I had to have you. On our very first date, I kissed you in the back seat of the limousine on the way back home. You couldn't resist me."

"No. *I* seduced you, on the way back home—" I insist, trying to gain the upper hand.

He goes on as if not having heard me.

Stubborn, arrogant man. Won't let me win even this one.

"We made wild, passionate, love in the back seat." His words arrow straight to my core. Dampness pools as my thighs clench.

I cross my legs.

A hint of a smile.

Damn him. Jace knows exactly what he's doing. He's using his words to turn me on.

"I woke you up the next morning, already hard and in you." His voice flows over me, sinking into my skin.

My eyes drop to his lap. He *is* hard. And aroused. He wants me. Makes no pretense of hiding it either.

How will it feel to have him inside me?

I shudder. Pin pricks of desire dance across my skin.

"You came home that night, and never left. That was a month ago. We've been together since." Jace's voice trails off.

I swallow, the sensations tumbling through me, nerves stretched to breaking point.

If he wanted he could have me now.

No. Fucking. Way.

"Relax," Jace says. "Get some rest while you can."

He pulls out the tablet again, bends over it with that absolute focus I'm coming to expect from him.

And I want to take the device from his hand and throw it away. Ask him to make me the focus of those incredible eyes

A shiver of anticipation, of liquid want spurts through my veins. *Stop it.* I tell myself. I'm beginning to hallucinate about this guy.

Sitting there next to Jace, in that enclosed space, the charisma coming off him in waves, I know I'm trapped.

7

———————

Sienna

Somerset Hotel, Hampshire, UK

The suite of rooms assigned to Jace is three times the size of my studio: two bedrooms with a living space and a kitchen in between.

When our bags arrived, I'd stalked into the main bedroom, laying dibs to the side of the bed I wanted to sleep on.

A small gesture. But it'd felt important to stake my claim as soon as possible. He may own my time but he can't control every single move I make.

I'd stalked into the shower, and when I'd emerged wrapped in a long bathrobe, he'd been on the phone, his back to the room, looking out the window, speaking to someone in a low voice.

Refusing to speculate who he was speaking to, I'd taken my gown and my cosmetics, and walked off into the other room to dress.

Now I turn to see myself fully in the mirror.

The green gown clings to my curves. When I move, the deep slit up one side parts enough to show a flash of my thigh. I can't get over how the dress dips in front, low enough to plunge almost to my navel. I'm not a prude, but jeans or formal trousers and a shirt are more my daily uniform.

I'm supposed to be alluring enough for a moneyed player, a cut throat investor like Jace, to fall for me.

I'd succeeded.

I look like... *sex*

Baring my teeth at my reflection, I stalk away from the mirror and pick up my small evening bag. Before I lose my nerve, I flounce out of the little room. My three-inch-high heels catch in the carpet, and I stumble.

Swearing aloud, I take a deep breath, then steady myself before walking across to the master bedroom. I fling open the door only to find the room is empty.

What the—? Where is he? So, I am late. *Only by half an hour.*

Turning away, I walk toward the kitchen and find a note propped up on the breakfast nook.

Downstairs, at the bar

It's unsigned.

For some reason, I'm angry he didn't wait for me. It's difficult enough being here, doing this. The least he could have done was walk me down.

Some moral support please?

Tearing it into tiny pieces, I drop it on the floor, then sweep out of the room.

When I reach the bar, it's empty.

Comfortable leather chairs are scattered around. I walk toward the sofa in front of a lit fireplace. I'm about to seat myself, when a draft from the half-open French doors makes me shiver.

I walk to the door and am about to shut it, when I spot Jace, his back turned to me. I lean out, trying to see who he is speaking to.

As I look on, Jace takes a last puff before stubbing out his cigarette. *He smokes?*

Except for what I've learnt from the Internet, I don't know much about him. Once again, the un-realness of my being here strikes me, and I shove at it.

Then the man opposite Jace, steps forward and comes into view. He's slimmer than Jace and ... he's beautiful.

Dark blond hair pulled back into a loose ponytail, with wisps escaping around his lean face. His skin is lighter than Jace's burnished brown, a pale olive color hinting at exotic undertones.

His startling violet eyes taper at the side. His cheekbones jut out, and a muscle twitches below one of them.

Jace turns as if to leave, and the other man reaches out, gripping his sleeve. He takes another step forward,moving close enough for his body to brush Jace. The other man says something, a frown marring that perfect forehead. He leans in even more and even at this distance I can see that this man feels a lot for Jace. That he wants to pull Jace close into his embrace.

It's as if he's already afraid of how Jace is going to react and yet he can't stop himself. As if he'll do anything for even a second more together.

Jace hesitates, then turning back, brings both arms around the man, hugging him close.

Feeling as if I am intruding, I move back toward the fire. I wrap my arms around my waist as a delayed chill from standing in the cool air outside sets in. A shiver runs down my back. I'm disturbed, and I'm not sure why.

It could've been just a friendly guy-hug.

But even as I'm thinking it, I know it isn't true. Whoever that man is, it's clear they know each other. Intimately.

Should I be shocked? After all, people do choose partners from both sexes.

But you haven't. You've never felt the need to sleep with another woman.

Not to say I've not been attracted to women, but I've never wanted to take it all the way.

But this is Jace. Sex-appeal-oozing Jace. A Jace who had undressed me with his eyes within seconds of meeting me the first time.

No. It doesn't feel right and yet, there's no mistaking the emotion on the other man's face. The one who'd clung to Jace as if his life depended on it.

My mind whirling at the possibilities and what this meant, I turn as if in a dream and walk to the sofa by the fire.

8

Jace

Asher's eyes burn into Jace. Familiar eyes that look through him, as if they want to swallow him whole.

It was inevitable he run into Asher here at Natalie's wedding. After all, Asher is still a part of London social circles. Regardless of the role Asher played in Jace's mother's death, Darren would still have invited Asher, if only to keep up appearances.

The emptiness of the life he'd opted out of comes crashing back. Silicon Valley was shallow too, but at least there, people were open in their drive to succeed and make money.

Yet, Jace had come, for he couldn't refuse his cousin. Natalie's the one person who knows why Jace left London after his mother died.

Seeing Asher had churned up those memories, never far from the surface. And landing in Heathrow and being surrounded by the familiar sights and smells had brought it all rushing back.

Perhaps his mother was right. There is no escaping one's past or one's destiny. She'd believed that.

But he'd never been *that* fatalistic, not till his life had turned upside down in the space of one night.

And the person responsible for all of it now is here, in front of him.

He'd wanted to push Asher away, to turn away and pretend he didn't know him. But seeing Asher in pain had made Jace pause. Asher is still grieving. For Jace's mother's death, for the friendship Asher and Jace once shared.

For the distance Jace had put between them.

Asher was in agony, his features twisted as if trying to hide his feelings, and failing.

Jace couldn't leave then. And when he'd finally looked into Asher's eyes, he was transfixed, transported back to the days after his mum's funeral, back to when he'd wandered his home in a daze, refusing to eat or drink till Natalie had come by. She'd told him to pull himself together. And even that hadn't helped.

As a child, Jace had often returned from school to find his mom sulking, refusing to see anyone. Not even her own son.

If she'd thrown a tantrum, told him off, or slapped him, he could have handled that.

But it was that indifference, that stoic sense of her putting up with him, that had pushed him over the edge. Even as a child, Jace knew, he hadn't mattered.

She'd done her job, hadn't she? Borne her husband an heir. And as far as she was concerned, that had been enough.

Perhaps everything Jace did in those growing years was to get a reaction from her.

Indulging Asher, leading him on when he had no intention of reciprocating Asher's affections, was a way of getting his parents' attention. But Asher's adoration had made Jace feel good.

With Asher, Jace could be as indifferent as he liked, as rude as he wanted. Jace could be himself and Asher would not leave. He'd known that deep inside.

Asher had mistaken his indifference for something deeper. He'd wanted Jace to become his lover.

Jace had turned him down, but by then it'd been too late. Asher was obsessed by Jace, would not let him go that easily. Asher had gone out of his way to get Jace's attention—with disastrous consequences.

Jace hadn't expected Asher to hurt him like that. Perhaps despite everything that happened between them, Jace had still considered Asher his close friend. And after what Asher did, Jace had simply withdrawn into himself.

It hadn't been Jace's style to throw tantrums. Unlike his father, who lost his temper at the least provocation, Jace had always been good at blanking people, cutting them out of his life completely, as if they never existed. A lot more like his mother than he'd cared to admit.

At twenty-two, Jace had opted to study in the US, going so far as to leave the continent itself behind.

It was only when Jace's mother committed suicide that he returned home, for the funeral. He'd stayed away again afterward.

Now Jace is back in London and facing Asher.

The past comes rushing back, and he can't stop himself from hugging Asher in the memory of his mother—the woman they'd both cared for in their own way. And lost. As if sensing his thoughts, Asher reaches up to wrap his arm around Jace's neck. He pulls his head down, and then kisses him.

Asher's loneliness pours into Jace, swimming through him. For a second, he can't move.

Then Jace pushes against Asher, breaking his hold. He steps back so quickly Asher's hands fall to his side.

Asher looks at him. Desire squeezes his violet eyes into pinpoints of black.

"Don't," Jace says. "What the fuck, man?" Anger explodes inside, his heart slamming against his ribs.

Asher holds up both his hands. "I'm sorry. Didn't mean for that to happen." The pain in his voice is evident.

"Just like you didn't mean to sleep with my mother. Like you didn't mean to push her to her death."

Jace is not sure why that slips out. He'd never known he'd miss his mother, not till she was gone.

Asher's face pales. He looks as if Jace punched him in the gut.

Turning, Jace strides away, through the French doors and toward the bar.

He can't put this off any longer. It's time to pay for his mistakes.

9

Sienna

A prickle of awareness ripples across my skin. Crossing the floor, Jace takes a barstool at the far end. His jacket clings to his shoulders, shows off his slim waist. He looks sleek, streamlined.

The bartender hands him a drink.

When Jace reaches for it, the makings of his tattoo peeks over the mandarin collar of his shirt. His back is erect, straight as if he's gathering strength to face whatever is in store.

He turns and meets my look head on. I flush, but don't turn away. *I will not turn away.*

I hold his gaze. Search for those familiar silver-green sparks in his eyes. Search for a clue that the man I saw outside, the one overcome with emotion, is the same cold, calculating man I'd met in Silicon Valley.

What I see instead is a man who is shattered. Jace is hurting. The stark loneliness in him reaches out to me, pulls at me. Before I realize it, I'm walking over to him without breaking that connection. I slip onto the barstool next to him.

When I gesture to his drink, the bartender places whiskey in front of me. I toss it back. The liquid burns its way down, and I cough. My eyes water, and I wipe away the tears. Then I sit there for another few seconds, letting my breathing stabilize.

Without waiting to be asked, the bartender tops up both our glasses.

This time, I clink my glass to Jace's without saying a word.

Our eyes meet for a second. Then he's drinking, tilting back the glass. He knocks back the drink, before I've even started on my second whiskey.

So, that's how it's going to be then? He wants to get drunk tonight. To numb the emotions he's feeling about the man outside.

I'd love to get drunk too. It's one way to forget how I came to be here, seated next to a man who has me at his beck and call for the next week. A man I find so attractive, and yet must resist.

If I sleep with him, I'll lose my own sense of self-worth.

I'm also aware that one of us needs to be sober here. Especially since it's technically 'meet the in-laws time' for me.

Changing my mind, I leave my drink untouched.

I am not sure what to say to him, though. I don't understand this strange, lost, almost vulnerable feeling vibrating off him. Almost as if he's half here and half not. As if he's reeling from shock. So, instead, I do something that surprises even me: I lace my fingers through his.

There's no reaction. He's silent.

Still.

And then he exhales in a quiet whoosh and grips my hand. Squeezing my palm, tangling his fingers through mine. I don't dare look up at him, don't want to see the expression on his face.

I sense he's not looking at me, either.

The bartender refills his glass.

His fingers tighten on mine. Without letting go of me, he uses his free hand to lift the refilled glass.

I'm sitting close enough to hear him gulp, sense the whiskey burn its way down his throat.

He shudders. "Thanks." His voice comes out rough, and he clears his throat.

"For what?" I look up and meet his eyes.

Lose myself in those silver-green depths.

Oh. My.

His gaze slide down my bare neck, and then farther down to where my dress stretches across my hips. I know the exact moment he sees the slit, showing most of my right thigh, for his jaw hardens. His gaze veers back up, tracing the plunging neckline.

Goosebumps on my forearms, and I try to pull my hand out of his grip to cover myself, but I can't.

His eyes lock with mine, that silver-green otherworldly fire sparking in them. He leans closer, so the side of his leg slides up against my thigh—the clothed one—and I gasp.

"What the hell are you wearing?" His voice is low, but firmer than a second ago.

He's angry. And that confuses me. The look in his eyes is so predatory, I shiver at the intent I read in them. When his palm squeezes mine, in a possessive gesture, pain shoots up my arm. I wince.

He still doesn't let go. Just stares at my lips.

He wants to kiss me.

Kiss me.

A strong curl of desire wells up inside. Rising, filling me. Overflowing till I'm sure it's bleeding from my fingertips into him.

Then, in a move that takes me by surprise, he raises his glass and touches the ice-cold surface to my neck.

I shiver.

His eyes are half closed. He knows that the contrast between the cold of the glass and the heat inside me is erotic.

And when a wave of heat washes over me, trickling down between my thighs, I'm sure he can feel that too.

His nostrils flare. Can he smell my arousal?

It's a rude reminder that I'm attracted to a man who'd been hugged by another guy as if his very life depended on it. Jace doesn't reciprocate the other man's attentions. And yet, I'm jealous.

"Why did you *really* want me to come here with you?" I blurt out.

Jace doesn't reply, merely stares into his drink. He's still gripping my hand.

I know then the reason I'm here, next to Jace, offering comfort, is to do with the man outside.

A burst of anger has me jumping to my feet. I tug my hand from his.

He lets me go so suddenly I fall back—right into the person standing behind me.

10

Sienna

Hands grip my upper arms, steadying me on my feet. I turn around, look up into a face I don't recognize.

Yet, something in the layout of those features is familiar. He's of medium height, stocky. Not even the tailored, tasteful suit he's wearing can quite conceal the bulge of muscles of his arms. His fingers holding me are thick, but gentle.

"Hey, Sienna." A wide grin lights up his pale brown eyes.

"Tom?" I gasp.

Am I dreaming? My childhood friend who I'd grown up with in Gainesville. The last time I'd seen him was before I'd moved to Silicon Valley. What's he doing in London?

Tom pulls me to him and kisses me straight on my lips.

Next to me Jace stiffens. Tension emanates off him. He hasn't said anything. And yet the space between us pulses with emotion. Jace's pissed off.

It makes me very conscious that I am standing here, in front of

Jace, within the circle of another man's arms. I hadn't set out to make him jealous. But a part of me is pleased.

"What are you doing here?" I ask, trying to wriggle out of Tom's hold.

"Sienna honey, you look amazing," he croons. Then he moves me back in position. Right. Against. Him.

I giggle.

It's a very Tom gesture. Over the top. Demonstrative. Not quite meaning it.

"What are you doing here?" I ask again, then answer my own question as I remember. "Your family did move to the UK, so I guess it's not a surprise you are in the country. But still, meeting you here?"

His hand works down to my butt, and I reach behind me to slap him away.

He'd always liked to flirt.

A pair of hostile eyes drill into me and I can't ignore Jace anymore.

Jace's eyes veer from me to Tom and back.

He doesn't move, but his hands fist at the side. The violence mixed with rage inside him reaches out to me, forcing me to react.

I push against Tom, pinch him in the arm till he releases me. Then I move back, till I feel the bar behind me. Putting enough distance between us, so it's clear we're not touching.

And yet, Jace doesn't take his eyes off us. That predatory look still in his eyes as if he's sensing something unspoken between me and Tom.

I want to explain that Tom is only a friend.

A childhood friend who means a lot.

And then I wonder, why do I want to do that? Why do I feel this need to calm Jace down, to provide an explanation?

As much as I want to tell him who Tom is, to clarify the situation, I also want to see Jace hurt. I want to see him helpless. As helpless as I'd felt watching him with that beautiful man outside.

The one I'm not going to ask about.

Tom looks from me to Jace, a question on his face. As if asking

Jace for permission? *Seriously?* Something passes between them. Something unsaid, a man-code of some kind.

Jace's eyebrows slash down. He lifts his hand and I flinch. But all he does is wrap his arm around my waist, hauling me close, the possessiveness in his gesture unmistakable.

Stunned, I turn to face him, as Tom's chuckle floats over my heads. "Who's your boyfriend, Sen?"

Damn. Tom is calling me by my nickname to annoy Jace. A not-so-subtle hint that Tom has known me for a long time. *Longer than Jace.*

"*Not* my boyfriend," I shoot back.

"Almost fiancé," Jace says in the same breath, his fingers tightening on my skin. He plasters me to his side.

And my emotions go a bit crazy inside. Why is Jace acting so possessive?

I like it. Very much.

Damn.

"Fiancé?" Tom's eyes dart to Jace, then back at me.

Feeling me stiffen, Jace brushes his hand over the bare skin of my lower back. The warmth of his body curls around me. His hand slips down to grip my hips and he hauls me to him. Fits me snugly into the 'V' between his legs. His arousal thrusts against the curve of my butt.

Oh. God.

Heat streaks through me, liquid desire. Moisture pools in my core. And my lips go dry.

I melt into him.

It earns us another stare from Tom, but I don't care.

I'm too busy trying to figure out what is happening between me and Jace. One minute, I think he's a cynical, money-minded man, trying to manipulate me. The next, he's showing a part of himself that I didn't know. A possessiveness that intrigues, that hints at something more between us.

The silence stretches.

Neither man makes the effort to introduce himself.

Tom turns to me, smiles. "Well then, why don't I leave you guys to it." Turning to me, he says, "I'm in room 208. Why don't we catch up later?"

Jace's muscles tense in response.

No, he didn't like the blatant invitation in Tom's voice.

I dig my fingers into his thigh. Rock solid muscle. I massage it and he stills.

Tom turns to go, then stops. "You're here for Natalie's wedding?"

"How did you guess?" I ask, then reply to my own question. "Of course, the entire hotel is booked out for the guests of the wedding, isn't it?"

Behind me the tension vibrating from Jace reaches a crescendo. Tom has outstayed his welcome. If he doesn't leave I'm sure Jace is going to do him bodily harm.

"Well then, guess we'll see you at the wedding?" I try to soften Jace's harsh dismissal of my friend.

A last tentative smile thrown in my direction, Tom leaves.

Jace and I stay as we are—my back against the unyielding strength of his chest. He fingers splayed across my belly. I feel the outline of each of his fingers through the thin material of my gown.

He's branding me.

A disturbing thought. More because it doesn't bother me as much as it should.

Damn.

I must tear myself away from him, move to straighten, and his arm tightens their grip on me. But when I take a step forward, he lets me go.

My heart lurches in disappointment.

Why do I like his touch on my skin so much?

Jace asks, "Did you know he was coming?"

I turn around, "I haven't seen Tom since I left home to move to Silicon Valley."

Jace nods, eyes hooded. He doesn't believe me.

11

Sienna

Jace and I cut across the hotel grounds. We head towards the pool house, where the evening cocktails are being held. I pause next to a bunch of pink flowers growing next to the garden path. Starlight lilies.

Bending down, I inhale deeply of their scent.

Soothing. It calms me a little.

I straighten, to see Jace watching me, eyes hooded.

"You like lilies?"

"Love their fragrance. They smell so exotic, intense with so many layers, it's almost like a puzzle." I keep my voice matter-of-fact. Another secret I've given away. I'm sharing more of myself than I intend to.

"You like puzzles?" He asks, voice husky.

"Hmm. Depends."

Are we still talking flowers?

My eyes skitter away to swimming pool that reflects the skies.

I don't want him to learn of my tastes. Any information he has will be used against me, I know that.

We continue walking.

The pool itself blends into the surroundings so artfully that the overall effect is natural. The unpretentiousness of it all hints at serious wealth. I've never felt so out of place.

Glasses clinking, the muted hum of conversation, and the sound of someone laughing floats across the balmy evening air.

We're about to be seen together as a couple, in front of other people. People who know Jace as the son to the heir of the Walker Fortune and a successful Angel Investor. *And they're going to find out that I am not what I seem.*

Fear jitters up my spine. I come to an abrupt stop. Jace continues a couple more steps before turning back.

He tilts his head, frowns.

"What is it? Is my tie askew?"

I shake my head, and the words stutter in my mouth.

The late evening breeze blows over my bare shoulders, and I shiver. That little scene with Tom has upset me more than I realized. And Jace's possessiveness has shaken me to the core. *I want more of the connection that had tied me to him.* It had made me feel I wasn't alone for the first time.

But this is a business relationship. He's employed me to play a role. And his being jealous of Tom was no doubt an act, a rehearsal for the façade we must maintain in front of his family.

Except I want it to be real.

I'm falling for him.

The breath catches in my throat. Emotions churn, tying my stomach in knots.

Can I get through this farce and get the money I need?

The thoughts I'd held at bay since I'd embarked on this insane trip come rushing over me. I feel a little sick as my mind lurches from one thing to another.

Leave now. Go.

I half turn.

Stop.

Turn back to him.

And perhaps in that slight jerky movement, in the flicker of uncertainty that scrolls across my face, he senses how close I am to breaking, to giving in and taking him to my bed.

Or letting him take me, possess me with that uncompromising need I sense in him. If we make love it won't be simple. Not simply a physical act. He'll want more. Demand I give him everything. My emotions. My feelings. He won't stop till he breaks through all the barriers. Strips me of my secrets. Owns every part of me.

Sleeping with him will mean giving up not only control of my business but also of my emotions. Never before has my independence, my sense of self been so threatened. I know our coupling will be nothing less than absolute, an act that will sear my soul.

I'm not ready for that.

Not yet.

His gaze sharpens and a look of concern shadows his features, gone so quickly I think I've imagined it. Then he closes the gap between us and he touches my cheek, pushing aside a strand of hair. A feather light touch that brings tears to my eyes.

"Hey," he says, his features uncomfortable, as if not quite sure how to handle this. "It's okay. If you'd rather not go in, we can head back up."

Swearing to myself, I screw my eyes shut to keep the tears from flowing.

Give me a demanding business negotiation, and I can face up to the toughest ball buster in town. But I'm useless when it comes to making sense of my own emotions.

I clench my palms at my side. He places his hand on my shoulder, and I freeze.

I don't look up, just focus on his throat. I want to reach out and place my lips there, find out how he tastes...and that confuses me even more. I'm in the middle of having a meltdown and all I can think of is touching this man. Biting my lips, I stand there frozen, unable to move. Knowing if I move I'd be lost.

Knowing if I don't leave now I risk losing myself in him. Only one day and I'm close to sleeping with him. If I spend a week with him, there'll be no turning back. I'll fall for him.

I'd lost my blood family, the ones I don't even remember. Then my adoptive father who had been the guiding force in my life. And now I'm in danger of falling for Jace. *Will he leave me too?* I'm merely someone employed to fulfill a role.

My emotions must have shown on my face, for he asks, "You aren't thinking of changing your mind, are you?" His voice is cautious.

I flinch.

Now that I hear him say it aloud, the foolishness of trying to get out of this arrangement hits me.

"As if that option is still open?" I say, and my voice comes out bitter.

He squeezes my shoulder. I wince again, this time from the real pain that shoots through my arm from his grip.

When I glance at him, I find his eyebrows furrowed as if he's trying to understand me, as if he's trying to figure out what to say. His eyes glint more silver than green in this light, stormy as if he's grappling with emotion.

"For fuck's sake, Sienna," he says. "Don't go getting cold feet now. I should have known. A novice like you wouldn't have the nerves to see this through."

I bristle. He's good at this, knows exactly which buttons to press.

"I'm not a novice," I say, my voice stronger as anger licks through my nerves.

He half-smirks and that only makes me want to prove him wrong.

I know he's playing me. Making me angry enough to take up his challenge and see this through. But even knowing he's manipulating me does not stop me from taking the bait.

Shrugging off his hand, I square my shoulders. Then, I stalk off toward the building by the poolside where the party is being held

12

Sienna

I push open the heavy black curtains leading into the pool house and step inside. The heat hits me, a contrast to the balmy evening outside, making me gasp. The stench of power, shot through with incense, overwhelms me.

Lit discreetly in the corners are glowing sticks stuck into the ground, bathing the space in notes of sandalwood and magnolia.

What looked like a two-floor Victorian structure from outside has transformed.

The space is big, much bigger than I would have imagined it to be. On one side an indoor pool—heated, judging by the steam rising off it.

On the far side women in swimsuits laze by the pool. One of them shrugs off her top. Dives in. Avid eyes follow her even as the conversation never ceases.

O-k-a-y.

Closer to me, men talk to each other. Men, with sculpted abs and tiny swimming trunks that reveal more than they hide.

One of them stops mid-conversation, catches me staring. I redden. Jerk my head to the other side.

There's a bar on the far end of the room. People scattered around, talking, holding drinks. The colored dresses of the women shimmer through the overheated air.

They look civilized, but I know they're not.

This is a genteel version of the Wild West. These men and women would tear each other's eyes out in their race to outdo each other. In money, possessions, their choice of sexual partner. One step wrong and they'll never let me live it down.

I. Don't. Care.

I refuse to be bogged down by the rules of this fake society. Or by Jace and his growing hold over my emotions.

A bead of sweat runs down between my breasts.

I hesitate, noticing the couple closest to me deep in conversation. The woman has a white, silk, shift dress, that clings to her every curve and leaves her shoulders bare. The man she's talking to is as tall as Jace, with grey hair at his temples.

His jacket stretches over his shoulders as he bends toward the woman. Even though his back is to me, something about the tilt of his head, the way he stands, is familiar. The woman looks over his shoulder, her eyes moving past me, to fix on someone else.

Jace. I feel his solid presence, next to me as he slips his arm around my waist. I barely stop myself from leaning on his strength.

The woman's face breaks into a smile, at which the older man turns. His eyes fall on Jace and pause with no change of expression. Before moving to me. Sweeping over me.

His gaze pauses on my breasts and my waist, sliding down my legs before snapping back to my face.

The audacity.

He walks toward us and I flinch. I'd have taken a step back, if it were not for Jace's arm, a steel band around my waist. His fingers splay, heat seeping through the material. He's trying to calm me.

I can't stop staring at the man approaching us.

Green eyes. Eyes familiar, yet different from Jace's. No trace of that silver that makes Jace so unique. No trace of life.

Yeah, Jace's eyes are alive, vital. Something I hadn't realized till now. In contrast this man's eyes are ice chips.

As the older man takes another step forward, there's no mistaking the threat, the anger implicit in every muscle on his frame.

Tension crackles between the two men. Conversation around us ceases. Everyone's watching, waiting. To see what happens next.

Caught in the crossfire, my heart stutters in fear. Then starts beating again. So fast I feel each. Individual. Heartbeat.

Jace's grip on me tightens. The pain cuts through my haze of confusion. He places a finger below my chin and turns my face to him.

"Look at me, Sienna," his voice is urgent, a frown marring his forehead.

I fix my gaze on the hollow of his neck, taking in a deep breath to steady myself.

The man stops beside us, but Jace doesn't acknowledge him. In a pointed snub, he bends down and brushes his lips over mine. Arm heavy around my waist, the other burning through the material on my shoulders, he hauls me to him, signaling his intent.

I am his. No mistaking the ownership.

Then Jace's tongue thrusts itself between my lips and I forget everything. The people watching us, the models by the pool. Everything fades.

Everything, except for the liquid fire that springs to life in my lower belly. The touch of his lips cuts to my core. Molten heat licks my nerve-endings.

I moan in my throat.

The sound is so erotic it makes my knees go weak. It also seems to remind Jace where we are. He raises his head, his eyes as stormy as the confusion inside me.

His palm slides down my back to rest on the curve of my waist.

Lips still throbbing from his kiss, I watch Jace turn around to the man who's been watching us all along.

"Hello, Father."

13

Sienna

"Quite a demonstration," Jace's father's voice slides over my skin. "You must be Sienna." The man holds out his hand. "I'm Darren."

His palm is rough, as if he spent the early years of his life in hard physical labor and now is trying to make up for it.

Dry warmth oozes into my blood. I shudder, tugging my hand. He lets go, then turns to Jace.

"So, the prodigal returns?" Sharp and cutting, the clipped English accent is underpinned by a rougher one I cannot place. Does he wear his mixed accent as a badge of his self-made status?

"It will take more than a kiss to show me that you're settling down." His voice is toneless.

No warmth between these two. Father and son are their worst rivals too.

Settling down?

"I'm here because Natalie asked me to come," Jace replies, his voice mild.

The woman Darren was speaking to comes up next to him.

"You made it." She hugs Jace, before pinching his cheek.

"You wanted me here." Jace smiles down at her. He bends down to kiss Natalie on her cheek, and then pinches her arm.

She giggles.

"Why don't you get Sienna a drink, gorgeous?" Darren asks the other woman. "Jace and I need to catch up. After all, it isn't every day a man sees his son after a five-year gap."

My gaze shoots to Jace.

Why hasn't he seen his father in so long?

Jace meets my eyes. His fingers caress my upper arm, before he lets me go with obvious reluctance.

Natalie chuckles. "Don't worry, cousin," She tells Jace, "I'll take care of Sienna."

I allow Natalie to pull me away. When I dart a last look over my shoulder, I find Jace and Darren walking out of the bungalow.

Natalie picks up two glasses of champagne off the tray of a waiter passing by, hands me one.

"To you," I toast her, raising the glass.

Natalie chuckles. "Aren't you a handful?"

I raise my eyebrows. *She has no idea how unpredictable I can be.*

Three glasses later, I'm collapsed on a couch. My head buzzing pleasantly.

The last time I got this smashed ... was with Tom, when he'd raided his father's stash of gin. He'd come over and we had proceeded to get drunk and sick.

Which is how my mother had found us. She'd grounded me for a week. Warned me against meeting Tom again. She'd never trusted Tom, never liked him even then.

The smoke from the incense in the space surrounds me, almost drugging me with the fragrance.

I look around, suddenly conscious that I don't know anyone else here.

Jace seems to have abandoned me, and Natalie ... well, she's standing only a few feet away from me, talking to her fiancé.

He whispers in her ear and she giggles. Then, she walks over to me. "Craig and I are gonna slip away. You'll be fine on your own?"

"Ah." I wiggle my finger in front of her. "Of course—" I hiccough,"—I am."

With a smile, she beckons one of the waiters to bring me water. Handing it over, she waits till I glug it down. Takes the empty water glass back and then says, "Tomorrow?"

"Tomorrow?" I blink.

"We're going shopping tomorrow, remember?" she says.

"Sure."

I'm thankful that she's been herself, a normal person to hang out with. A relief after those strained, chemistry-charged moments that always seem to hang between me and Jace.

Leaning over, I kiss her smack on her lips.

Oops.

"You'll make Craig jealous." She giggles. "You sure you'll be okay?"

"Of course." My voice is vehement, but she doesn't seem convinced.

I reach for another glass of champagne from a passing waiter only to have her rap me on my knuckles.

"Hey."

I pull back, fingers curled.

When she raises her eyebrows in warning, I shut up.

"I'll find Jace and send him to you. You stay right here, and remember we are meeting at the hotel lobby tomorrow." With a last warning look, she leaves.

I hiccough, but stay on the couch.

The crowd has grown considerably over the past hour. The heat is suffocating, pressing in on my skin. Sweat breaks out on my brow, and I wipe it off. A shout from the swimming pool draws my attention there, in time to see a man and woman fall into it, their lips still locked.

Even as a warning goes off in my head, I'm up and moving toward the pool.

14

———————

Sienna

By the time I reach the edge of the pool, the world is whirling around me. I grab the thing closest to me to steady myself, which turns out to be a man. One I recognize.

He's tall and lean, with broad shoulders. He grins as he steadies me, his hands lingering on my forearms.

Violet eyes look down at me.

He's built like a model.

Seeing him in these brief swimming trunks stretched across his front pings a message to my head.

Hell, he *is* a model. An underwear model. One well-known, too, given I now recall seeing his face in many magazines. And he's holding my arms, looking at me as if he wants to take me to bed.

Except I've seen him with Jace. Know he feels something for him. He'd looked at Jace as if he was still in love with him.

And I'm perilously close developing an attraction for Jace, too.

He wipes the drop of sweat that trickles down my temple.

"Fancy a dip to cool off?" he says in a pronounced American drawl.

I resist the urge to roll my eyes. I know a bad pick up line when I see one, even when I am tipsy.

He grins down at me. The skin crinkles at the corner of his eyes. He's perfect. Too perfect—enough to make me want to reach out and touch his cheek to check that he is real.

He slides his finger down my arm.

"Well, what do you say, gorgeous? You ready to take a dip and show these people exactly what a party is all about?"

What's he talking about?

Before I can ask, he turns. Dives into the pool, with barely a ripple. Surfacing a few feet away he calls out, "Come on in."

What? He's crazy. My eyes dart around the pool, at the interested crowd watching us. They know I'm Jace's girlfriend.

One wrong move will cause Jace to lose face in front of his family. Worse it means I break our arrangement and I'll lose the money needed to secure my future.

I hesitate.

"Lost your nerve?" The beautiful man from the pool calls out, treading water.

His features are serious, assessing. All lightheartedness gone from the moment.

He's daring me.

That's the second person tonight to accuse me of that.

A fine spark of rage shivers up my spine. The one thing I can never resist is a challenge. I've always followed my heart. It's what had made me move to Silicon Valley pursuing of a crazy dream.

It had made me determined to put Bella through school disregarding the odds.

Bella.

Thinking about my sister gives me pause for thought. She's the reason I'd thrown caution to the wind and accepted Jace's insane proposal.

Now, that same recklessness pushes me toward the edge of the pool. Beneath it all, I'm still smarting from his taking control of my life since we met.

This is my chance to show Jace he cannot influence my every move. We've come this far, people know of me as his girlfriend, it's too late for him to turn back too. He too has no choice but to see this through with me.

And hadn't that other woman taken off her bikini top and jumped in too?

My heart beats faster, the blood thunders in my ears.

Without giving myself a chance to change my mind, I reach down for the hem of the dress and pull it up. All the way up and over my head, dropping it. The expensive materials falls in the water.

Braless, and clad only in a thong, I dive in. Surface, gasping. My head already clearing. Everything seems brighter, sharper.

Shaking the hair out of my face, I laugh. Adrenaline pulses as a feeling of being free shoots through my blood.

I feel naughty. Very naughty.

I laugh again, then splutter as I swallow water and go under.

An arm reaches out, and the man who'd dared me to jump in surfaces with me clutched in front of him.

"You okay?"

I nod, eyes watering, before sputtering, "Now look what you've done. I'm going to be in so much trouble for this."

I grin, giddy with the adrenaline coursing through me. I am going to pay for this, and yet, I can't stop myself from laughing aloud at the wickedness of the moment.

"Seems I've misjudged you," he chuckles.

"Seems many have misjudged me," I shoot back.

"Oh?" He raises his eyebrows.

Just like that, he reaches down and brushes his lips across mine. The same lips that had kissed Jace, not many hours ago.

The thought is enough to make me lose my balance again. He grips me tighter, steadying me.

When I think things can't get any worse, I hear my name being called. Turn to see Jace striding toward us.

An *infuriated* Jace.

Those silver-green eyes blazing fire.

Fuck.

Asher's grip on me tightens, and he glances from me to Jace and then back at me. He's not surprised. *He'd been counting on Jace finding us like this.*

A mix of emotions I can't quite interpret twists the guy's features and then his eyes widen. He swims toward the far end of the pool away from Jace, then turns, waiting for me to follow.

A prickle of unease runs down my spine. Something's going on here and I can't quite put my finger on it.

A part of me wants to get out of the pool, go up to Jace and apologize.

But that other crazy part of me, the one that never stops to think, the one that always dares me to try new things is in heaven.

I swim away from where Jace is standing and toward where the model is holding up a towel for me. *I'm going to pay for this.*

15

Sienna

Jace's friend helps me out of the pool, and then slips his shirt over my shoulders.

"You want a drink to warm up?" He asks.

I look up from buttoning my shirt. "Now?"

My eyes are drawn to where Jace is watching us from the other side of the pool. He turns to circumnavigate the pool. He's headed toward us. But I don't trust myself with him. Not the way I am feeling right now.

Rebellious, slightly drunk. And with the adrenaline of the dip in the pool still thrumming through my veins.

If Jace touches me now, I'll want to make love with him.

Wild, passionate, love.

Suddenly a drink with anyone else sounds like a good idea.

If I do this, if I go with Asher now, I know it will push Jace over the edge. I want to find out how far I can push him, before his control snaps.

I turn toward the model waiting for me.

"Wait." I hesitate, "What's your name?"

"Asher."

"Sienna."

"I know." He tilts his head.

Of course he knows who I am. Knows too that I'm using him to bait Jace. Perhaps Asher, too, wants this confrontation.

I dart one last look over my shoulder, to see Jace pick up my now soaking-wet dress.

Past him, at the far end of the room, Eric looks at me, his features frozen in near comical surprise.

16

____

Jace

Jace had entered the pool house looking for Sienna, knowing he'd been away for too long. The meeting with his father had, as usual, left him feeling inadequate and angry.

People mellowed with age, but not his dad.

The man was hell-bent on cheating the aging process. His father worked out every day. Took anti-oxidants and supplements to keep his energy levels up.

Each of his wives was younger than the last, as if he was trying to absorb the vigor of the younger women who still flocked to him.

His current wife—number five to be precise—was only five years older than Jace. Thirty-five to his father's sixty.

And when Jace had originally asked for his inheritance, Darren had been very clear. He was willing to bail him out one last time, provided ... he came back and joined the family business. And while at it, he had to get married and produce an heir, to carry on the Walker name.

And seeing Asher in the pool with Sienna had pushed him over the edge.

Rage had whipped through Jace, surprising him in its intensity. Reaching the edge of the pool, his foot had brushed the dress that was half in water.

Now, as he stands there, he knows she is baiting him. Forcing him to look her in the eye and tell her off, tell her to leave, to remove herself from his life.

He isn't having any of it.

She isn't getting away that easily.

Sienna hauls herself out of the pool, sliding into the shirt Asher drapes around her almost immediately.

But not before he and every other man in the room gets an eyeful of her bare ass. Her curved, smooth, round ass. Barely covered by a flimsy thong, it flared up to meet the hollow of her back.

A noise from the side and he turns to see his father right behind him, his eyes riveted to the scene. Darren's chest rises and falls erratically. He is turned on. Jace hopes to God he has a heart attack.

A giggle draws his attention back to where Asher is leading Sienna to the opposite exit. Jace hasn't been able to take his eyes off her. The sway of her butt under the shirt. And her hair, now wet, hints of copper glinting among the thick strands.

Now Sienna turns and throws one last look at him over her shoulder.

A dare.

She's daring him to follow her.

To find her.

His fist entangled in the wet, green dress, he turns to come up against his father.

Darren's eyes snap at him with anger, and below that, the never far away boredom. The one that Jace has faced all his life.

"After that stunt your girlfriend pulled, I am tempted to disinherit you right now, but I won't. Not yet."

"To what do I owe that honor?" Jace snaps, not in any mood to tangle with Darren just then.

"I know you think I'm being unfair in the conditions I've imposed on you. But one day, perhaps when you are a father yourself, you'll know why I did it."

It's the first time in all the time Jace's known him that Darren's hinted at his awareness of his own role as a father. Yet, Darren's always taken position as the patriarch to the extended family seriously. After his brother's death, he's ensured the future of his niece, Natalie.

But with his son—his only child—he's always been uncompromising. A part of Jace even recognizes the wisdom in that. That his father is trying to teach him discipline that will hold him in good stead in the future. And yet, that boy inside him who'd hungered for his father's love still resents the heavy hand with which his father had controlled his life.

Exactly how Jace is trying to control Sienna's.

Jace couldn't stop his parents from destroying each other. So, he'd instead turned to controlling his own life and the people in it. He'd succeeded so far.

Until Sienna came along and challenged all his notions. He thought he could use her need for money to his advantage. Been confident she'd do exactly what he wanted.

But she'd shocked him out of his complicity.

She'd jumped in that pool, almost naked. Then walked away with Asher.

The same Asher he'd turned down in the past. He can't get his head around that.

And then Jace realizes then why he's so angry. It's not at Darren, or even at Asher for what he'd done.

It's because Sienna makes him feel emotions he's long buried inside. Jace has spent years living fast and loose, shallow. Trying to control the people around him. He's spent his life trying to prove that like Darren, he too can be a self-made man. All of this to win Darren's approval.

Now, on the verge of his own ventures failing, he's back at Darren's doorstep, back for the same millions he's spent his life running from. For that's the only thing that can save him from bank-ruptcy. From losing face in front of the world.

Yeah, he's his father's son all right. He'll do anything to maintain the veneer of success to the external world. Even manipulate the only person who's held up a mirror to him, shown him who he has become.

Jace's anger fades away, replaced with jealousy. Sheer, gut-wrenching jealousy. He's going to find her and get her away from Asher.

As he turns to leave, Darren's voice stops him.

"You have one more chance to bring your...girlfriend to heel. To show you are serious about settling down." Darren says. "That there is something more than merely lust between the two of you. I want you to have what I never found."

"Have what? True love?" Jace asks, his voice sharp with disbelief.

"Peace," his father replies. "I want you to find yourself, Jacob."

Jace's head snaps up at that. No one called him by his given name. Except his father.

Darren had done so only when he was furious with his son, or when...he was overcome by emotion. The last time was at his mother's funeral. When his father had hugged him.

Now Jace is grown. And yet inside, a part of him is still that confused boy. Perhaps that part will always be a boy thirsting for his mother's love, his father's approval. Yet, for the first time, Jace looks past his father's faults. To the iron will inside. His father cares for him in his own way, wants him to become his own man.

Unorthodox as his methods may be.

Jace tilts his head, nods.

Then without another word, he turns, and stalks toward the exit.

Now, though, he must find Sienna. Get her away from Asher.

As Jace heads for the door, Eric walks up to him to lay a hand on his sleeve. Jace shakes him off.

To his surprise, Eric grabs his hand and turns him around, letting go almost immediately when Jace trains his eyes on him.

Eric holds his ground. "Go easy on her."

"*You* keep your hands off her." Jace snarls back before he can stop himself.

Holding up both his hands to show he means no harm, Eric says, "Don't see a ring on her finger that indicates she is yours. Besides, after what she did today, every man in the room wants her, will probably pay to have her for his mistress."

He's right.

No fucking way is that going to happen. Sienna belongs to him and he is going to make sure everyone here gets that message loud and clear.

Jace doesn't stop to wonder when the business arrangement between him and Sienna turned so personal

17

Sienna

Asher's room in the hotel is not even half the size of the suite I share with Jace. I am shivering from the walk through the garden. The cool air has also cleared my head a little, bringing with it a dawning realization of what I've done.

The one chance I had to get the money and rescue my business and I've blown it. That's it, then. I can kiss the money from Jace goodbye. I swear inwardly.

I had taken up Asher's challenge to follow him into the pool. Worse. *I. Had. Stripped. Bare.* In front of all the guests.

I cover my face and groan aloud.

As if that were not enough, I'd made sure Jace had seen me leave with Asher. Had dared him to follow. I had provoked him.

And I can't understand why I'd done it.

Because I'd been drunk? Too far gone to care about the reason I had come here in the first place? No, that's not true. I knew what I'd been doing.

I'd goaded Jace. I'd wanted to get him to react, to find out if he feels anything for me.

I wanted to provoke him. Make him feel jealous. Wanted to make him feel the way I do when I see him. Make him want me the way I want him.

And I'd also been jealous of the emotions I'd seen on his face as he talked with Asher at the hotel.

Somewhere in the last few days, I'd begun to want this man. The need to possess him is slowly taking root.

I'd let the lust inside come to the fore. And now I am going to pay for it.

Jace's going to walk away from the bargain, and I am going to lose everything.

As these thoughts run through my head, Asher looks at me and says, "Why don't you take a shower? You look cold."

I purse my lips. "Are you also going to use that line with me?"

"Why?" He asks, his face expressionless. "Is that what *he* said to you?"

I don't need to ask who Asher is referring to. There is only one 'he' as far as we're both concerned.

Without bothering to reply, I walk into toward the bathroom.

"Wait," he calls out before I can shut the door.

He rummages around in the chest of drawers by the wall near the bathroom, before handing me a pair of jeans, shirt, a belt.

I walk out after the shower with the jeans rolled up almost double. It's held up by tying the belt twice around my waist.

Asher has changed too. He's bare-chested, and wearing comfortable pajama bottoms. They mold to his thighs and hang around his hips. Sculpted chest and a flat stomach. Well defined muscles, angle down into a 'V' toward his groin area.

Once again, he looks to have stepped straight out of a fashion advertisement. This man is gorgeous.

Too perfect.

Unlike Jace, who has a rougher, more natural appeal. The kind I prefer to the manufactured prettiness on display in front of me now.

"You look good." Asher says.

"No way." I laugh, running my hands through my damp hair which lies in raggedy tails around my face.

"You don't know your own appeal, do you? Perhaps that's what Jace likes."

I stare in disbelief, and he chuckles. Walking to the bar, Asher pulls out a bottle of whiskey, pours two glasses. A good-sized portion of the golden-brown liquid from the bottle disappears into the glasses.

"Here."

I walk toward him, taking the offered glass.

"What should we drink to?" he asks.

I look from him to the glass, then back at him. "To Jace."

His eyebrows shoot down over his nose, before his eyes crinkle. "To Jace's girlfriend."

He clinks his glass to mine, throws the liquid down his throat.

When he slams his glass back on the table, his hand is unsteady. He's not as calm as he seems.

I recall again the look on his face when Jace had turned away from him outside the bar.

Something doesn't quite add up, but I can't put my finger on it. Then that thought too fades as Asher walks to the bed in the center of the room. He flings himself on one end, on the covers. Pats the space next to him.

I hesitate.

"Do I have to dare you once more?" A wicked smile lights up his face. "Besides, I'm harmless. *Relatively.*"

His eyes fall on my lips, travel down to the thrust of my breasts.

Desire shimmers off him.

It surprises me, the sexuality that swirls around this guy. It's like he's wearing a cloak, a tangible, living, breathing need that moves with him. A vivid image of Asher pulling Jace to him flashes across my mind.

Asher is still in love with Jace. And he'd invited me to his room, and now he's trying to seduce me. Why?

A frisson of disquiet runs down my spine.

Harmless, my ass.

Still, I can't help but be impressed at his audacity. He knows I'm Jace's girlfriend, that Jace would hardly be pleased by what he's done.

Asher'd thumbed his nose at the entire Walker clan. Sent a clear signal to them that he didn't care about their money, or their prestige. And for that, at least, I admire him.

As the adrenaline from the evening wears off, a slight drowsiness creeps over me.

"I should go back to my own room."

I don't turn to leave. Don't move toward the bed either.

"You don't want to be alone tonight." Asher's voice is soft, unthreatening. He folds his arm behind his head, throwing his chest in sharp relief.

The thought of going back to my own room *is* unappealing. I've already burnt my bridges with Jace. Nothing I do can make it worse.

Can it?

Besides, I'm tired. As I think that, a wave of fatigue washes over me. I want to take the weight off my legs. It won't matter if I lie down.

I walk around the bed and, placing my still-filled glass on the side table, flop on the other side of the bed. As far away from Asher as possible.

We sit there for a few seconds and when he doesn't make any further move to reach out to me, my muscles begin to relax.

"So, how did he get you to do this?" he asks.

I pause, take a sip of my own drink.

"Do what?" I ask, my voice innocent.

"You know exactly what I mean."

"Jace is my boyfriend," I say, not looking at him.

"Right," he says in a voice that implies he doesn't believe me at all. "So what are you doing here with me, Sienna? In the middle of the night."

I exhale a soft breath, not replying. I don't know what to say. Not when even I'm not sure why I am doing this. What's compelling me to do everything possible to anger Jace. Do I resent what he's making me feel? That he's making me want him. Even as I know everything he's pretending to feel for me is a sham. There's no way our relationship can ever become a reality.

In the silence that follows, Asher places his glass down with a snap. The sound cuts through the thoughts whirling around in my head.

Asher rolls over, bridging the distance between us. Before I can react, he flings his body over mine, imprisoning me.

I edge back against the pillows, my head hitting the headboard.

He's close enough now for me to make out the individual lines at the corners of his eyes. The fine lines on his forehead, barely covered by the dark blond hair that falls over it in waves. It cascades down to below his shoulders.

Without meaning to, my gaze tracks down his bare chest. And further down to the unmistakable swell of where his erection presses against the thin material of his pajamas.

It's almost like he's drawn the best from both genders. Masculinity tempered with a smoother, more tender feel around the edges.

He lifts his eyes to my face. Hooded eyes, half closed now and shining. Heat spools off him, curling around me again. So, different than the more aggressive warmth from Jace.

Eyes glittering, Asher moves closer. His pulse beats faster, the skin at the base of his throat jumping, as his breath brushes over my lips.

His eyes swivel up to meet mine, in them I see a question and curiosity.

18

Sienna

Asher's head descends toward me. I turn away at the last moment. His lips brush my cheek instead.

"You smell good," he brings his nose to the hollow of my neck, sniffs. Adds in a thoughtful voice, "Earthy, almost chocolaty, and yet there's something ... a spicy undertone."

He brushes his nose against my skin.

"Don't." My voice comes out breathless.

He stares into my eyes, his violet irises so vivid they feel electric.

I push against his shoulder trying to put some distance between us when there's a knock on the door.

Asher lets go, leans back.

My breath catches in my throat and my heart slams against my ribs as I stare at Asher, my eyes wide with shock.

I know who it is.

But Asher is already sliding over me. His feet hit the floor with a thud. His face is smooth. Calm.

I'd been expecting Jace to come here searching for us. It's why I'd let Asher play me all along. Been his willing accomplice in creating this set up for Jace to walk in on.

Asher walks to the door. Opening it, he steps aside, letting Jace see me. In Asher's bed. Wearing Asher's clothes.

Looking flushed, as if we've been making love.

Jace comes to an abrupt halt. Asher grips his arm and pulls him in. Jace doesn't even notice. He hasn't taken his eyes off me. And I'm watching him, too.

Jace's features are frozen. Eyes narrow, liquid silver. Emotions race across his face, before he blanks his face completely.

A mask.

If I'd thought he'd been difficult to read before, now he feels unreachable.

"Why don't we—" Asher begins, only for Jace to put up a palm, stopping him mid-sentence.

Asher stops, a hurt expression twisting his features. Asher still cares for Jace. That's why he asked me to his room. To make him jealous.

I almost laugh aloud.

Both Asher and I had the same goal in mind. To use each other to get Jace's attention.

Well, we've succeeded.

A shiver of apprehension runs down my spine.

Jace turns and walks out.

And that hurts.

Like I've hurt him.

Silence.

Sliding from the bed, I force myself to put one foot in front of the other. To walk out of the room and catch up with Jace.

We stay quiet as we walk through the garden. My bare feet press down on the stones, pebbles scraping my feet. I wince, but keep moving. When I stumble, almost fall, Jace doesn't even look back. He can't bear to touch me.

My heart twists.

I deserve it.

Reaching the main building, we walk through the deserted lobby, up a staircase to our suite.

The door whispers shut.

Jace stalks to the window, looks out, hands thrust into his pockets, his back a solid, impenetrable wall of muscle.

Seconds stretch. Slide into minutes. Beyond him, the window looks out on a darkened piece of night.

As dark as the atmosphere in this room.

And we still stay as we are.

I shiver, goose bumps on my skin, becoming aware too I'm still dressed in Asher's clothes.

Fuck.

I know when I'm being punished.

I'd been curious what he'd do if I broke every rule. Broke through the walls he'd built around him.

I'd expected him to be angry, to rage at me. Perhaps even try to take me to bed. Either way I'd hoped to feel his emotions. Find out if he feels for me.

I hadn't expected him to completely blank me like this. Pretend I don't exist.

Unable to bear it, I finally break the silence, "I didn't sleep with him."

He doesn't turn around.

Nothing.

A sliver of anger at being ignored ripples down my spine. I hurt him, I am not the injured party here. And yet, I've had enough. I want to force a reaction from him.

I walk to him, reach out a hand. Let it fall to my side without touching him.

I'd been mistaken. He's not withdrawn or blanking me.

He's not *just* angry.

He's... livid.

The rage leaps off him, crackling the air around him. I realize then how big a mistake I've made.

I'd wanted to see the man behind the walls he'd put up to the world. Nothing has prepared me for what I'm about to unleash.

I take a step back, but it's too late.

He turns, snaps his eyes on mine. Gold sparks among the silver-green. I've pushed him over the edge.

The anger inside him is a living, breathing thing that threatens to pounce on me. Fear and … desire curl in my belly, taking me by surprise.

I see the rawness of this man for the first time. Face that part of him he's kept caged so far. And I'm not sure I'm ready for it.

I also sense something beyond anger. Hurt. I've hurt this man. Let him down in front of his family.

Sure, he'd brokered a deal with me, but at some level he'd also put his future in my hands. He'd trusted me.

I'd acted like a rebellious child and broken his trust.

And when I'd seen him with Asher, I'd been so jealous. I'd realized then I couldn't bear to see him with anyone else. Hated him at some level for making me want to care for him, despite the control he had over my future.

And then I couldn't stop.

Well, now I've ruined everything. For him. For me.

I'd expected to feel satisfied at showing him up, but all I feel is regret.

For the first time since I met him, I wish there was a chance for us to have met in different circumstances. Not like this, when there's a business transaction between us.

I must make amends. And perhaps at the end of all this I'll have to walk away to my broken life with nothing to show for it. So, be it. The least I can do now is apologize.

"I'm sorry," I murmur. "I shouldn't have let you down."

Jace's eyes widen, but there's no other reaction on his face.

Instead he says something that surprises me. "Stay away from Asher." His voice is soft but the violence beneath, unmistakable.

"Jealous?"

A flare of hope leaps to life.

His jaw hardens, a vein beating at his temple. "Asher's unpredictable."

"More than me?" I ask.

It doesn't even draw a chuckle from him.

I flush.

"He'll hurt you, like he hurt my mother." His voice is hard. "He was only twenty-one when he seduced her. He slept with my mother, for fuck's sake. I walked in on the two of them, in my bed. But even that didn't stop her from falling in love with him. He was using her to get my attention. And when Asher turned her down, my mother killed herself."

The words come rushing out and I recoil.

He'd walked in on me and Asher exactly as he had walked in on Asher and his mother. I can't even begin to understand how that must feel. The hurt radiates from him, and I cringe.

The full repercussions of my actions hit home.

I not only broke our agreement, but made him relive the worst nightmare of his life.

19

____

Sienna

"I am so sorry," I whisper. It sounds so inadequate.

I'd betrayed him, and before those who mattered to him. Now all I can feel is this compulsion to put things right.

"Let me make it up to you," I say, my voice soft.

His nostrils flare. Can he sense the conflicting emotions inside me?

The fury on his face gives away to a more assessing look. His eyes narrow, giving him a predatory aspect—one I associate with the Jace I'd heard about by reputation—the spoilt, eccentric multi-millionaire.

His eyes sear a path down my body, touching on the hollows of my throat, over my breasts, dipping down my waist, between my legs.

His intent clear.

I know he wants me.

I've been drawn to Jace from the moment I set eyes on him. I want to take him to bed. But is sleeping with him a last-ditch attempt to salvage our arrangement? *So, I can still get the money.*

I hesitate, unsure what to do.

When his eyes drop to my lips I shiver.

He waits. The moment stretches till I can't take it anymore.

He's waiting for me to make the first move. Patience has never been my strong point.

I stand up on tip-toe, touch my lips to his. Just a brush.

My eyelids flutter down.

That pine and clove smell of his surrounds me, drawing at me, coaxing me to get closer.

Heat spirals out from him, twisting around me, and I moan in my throat. The vibrations ripple toward my breast, hardening my nipples and down further, joining the liquid space between my legs.

Still he doesn't move.

My eyes fly open, and the breath catches in my throat. Those silvery-green pools shimmer with hunger. But his expression is calm, his features almost relaxed.

He's still waiting.

Waiting for me to show him. That I'm ready for him.

Ready for 'this,' whatever it is.

There's also a warning in his gaze. He's holding himself back. If he lets go this time, nothing can stop him.

I hesitate, only a millisecond. But his eyes widen, and then the silver-green turns opaque, as if all the emotions have leached out from it. His jaw hardens and tension vibrates from him.

I can't take it.

Can't take this indecision that's crawling through me, making my head whirl with repressed feelings. I'm afraid. And excited. And shocked at my arousal. At how turned on I am by this man's presence.

Leaning on tip toe, I brush my lips across his. Once. Twice.

No response.

I deepen the kiss, thrust my tongue through his lips, forcing his mouth open.

He takes a step back to rest his hips against the window ledge. I move with him.

Hands by his side, he's still not kissing me back.

I pull away and his gaze narrows, bringing back that hunter's look to his face. The skin stretched over his cheeks makes them look even more prominent. Feral.

He's daring me. Challenging me to seduce him.

And when I lean in this time, those silvery-green are unbearably close. It makes me want to blink under the full onslaught of his emotions. Anger. Betrayal...Lust.

An explosive combination.

Scratching my nails up his arm, over his jacket, I bite down on his lips, sliding my tongue over them, slowly.

Our eyes war. Mine angry, his stormy.

But he doesn't make a single move.

Fuck.

In a last-ditch attempt, I close the remaining space between us, so we're touching from chest to groin to thigh. Sliding my hands around his neck, I plunge my fingers through his hair, gripping the strands and bringing his head down to mine.

I let my emotions come to the fore. Let the part of me I've closed off well up—the confusion of moving to this country, the pain of my adoptive father's death, the need to protect my mother and sister, the thrill of finally being independent. I let myself show.

Me.

I pour myself into the kiss, the way I've never done before. Not to anyone else.

And then I'm spent.

The rush of adrenaline drains away, leaving me shivering and disappointed. I'd been trying to get through to him, to get him to see me on my own terms ... and failed.

I need to leave while I can. My hands drop to my side. I turn my head to move away, only to have his arms snake down around my waist.

He hauls me to him. Heaves me up, so my feet spring off the floor to wrap around him.

All thoughts escape, as his lips crush mine, arms encircling, holding me to his chest. He devours me with his mouth and I'm dimly aware of him moving.

I don't want to close my eyes. Can't stop drinking in the flush of desire racing a blush across his cheeks and evident in his arousal that throbs against me. Wanting me.

The world tilts as he lowers me to the bed. His body covers mine, his weight pushing me down into the bed.

Drawing my hands over my head, he shackles them with his fingers around both my wrists. His other hand runs over my breast, down my waist, and across my hips, squeezing in a possessive gesture.

I gasp aloud, the sound swallowed by his mouth.

Liquid heat shoots through me, slamming my heart against my ribs.

As if in response, he releases my hands and raises himself on his arms, biceps bulging, and leans forward, my legs still wrapped around him. Taking hold of the gaping ends of my shirt above my breast, he rips it open so the buttons go flying. I gasp in shock. A ripple of excitement coils deep in my belly, making me arch up toward him. I moan a little as the sheer unexpectedness of my desire makes me tremble.

The next thing, he's shrugging off his shirt, and I can't stop staring. I know he's in good shape... but this.

Oh, God.

He's beautiful.

Sculpted chest, a flat stomach that slopes down to his pants. His erection hard and pushing against the material. The heat pulsing off him is so tangible, my throat goes dry.

I raise my eyes back to the tattoo I had seen peeking above the collar of his shirt.

I run my hands over his muscles, over lines of black script in Hindi flowing over his upper arm, and shudder.

It's the last place I'd expected to find a connection to my birth-place, the one I'd left behind and sworn never to look back at.

Now, finding it on the skin of this man who had, for all purposes, come forward to help me, makes me feel I'm caught in a strange web that's tightening its hold around me.

Goose bumps spring up on my back, and I shiver, pressing myself closer to him.

If I lose myself in him, can I forget where I come from? Forget my responsibilities to my company, to my family, even if it's for a little while?

I press my palm flat against his skin, feeling the contours, the shape of those muscles, the curves, dips, and hollows. The heat from his skin bleeds into my fingertips, down my arm, and arrows in straight for that sweet spot in the groin.

I swallow, and his eyes dart to my throat, then my lips. Then he leans down and kisses me again, his hand running up my thigh, sliding around to press between them.

Fire bursts through my veins.

He runs a finger over my core through the borrowed pants I'm still wearing. Then, unbuttons the pants, yanking them down my thighs. I slide my legs from around him, only long enough for him to fling them off.

I kick off my panties, and before I've drawn a breath, or thought about how I look through his eyes, he bends down again and kisses my lips, drawing from me so deeply, my head spins.

He lets go, only to kiss my shoulder. He bites down until I gasp. His hand cups my breast, squeeze the nipple and goose bumps erupt all over me. I lower my arms only to have them captured and pushed back.

He shackles them with strong fingers, holding me captive, trailing his other hand down my belly. Lower still.

Writhing under his touch, I gasp, "Let me touch you."

In reply he thrusts his finger inside me.

Mercy.

I jerk, crying out, raising my hips off the mattress, but he doesn't give. Not even a little. Just follows it up with another finger, filling me. In and out again. Thrusting in so deeply my eyes roll back in my head with the sheer heat that crashes through me.

I can barely feel myself, or him, or what his fingers are doing to me.

What is *he* doing to me?

I swear at him, straining against his hold, my bare legs trapped under his. Skin rasping against the cloth of his pants.

My helplessness only adds to his arousal.

And that only makes me strain against him more even as I come against his hand. The intensity of the sensation smothers me, firing my nerve endings so every pore in my body is crying out with pleasure.

By the time I recover from the sexual haze, he's pulling off me. He withdraws from me mentally and emotionally, his body rolling off me as he slides to his feet, still wearing his formal trousers. His face is an unreadable mask.

He brings his fingers to his lips, licks.

And that moves me even more than having his mouth on me. It feels curiously intimate, as if he's wearing my essence, tasting it.

Feeling myself go wet, I sit up and reach for him, but he steps away.

The heat pulls back from over me, as if being sucked right back into his body. I shiver, aware for the first time that I am not wearing clothes.

Some of the desire fades. His breathing is normal too. The predatory look is gone from his eyes, leaving them more silver than green.

He reaches for his discarded shirt, slipping it on. Leaving it unbuttoned he walks away from me.

My pulse hammers as I try to make sense of what's happening.

"Wait," I call out. "Why?"

He doesn't even look back.

"Why?" I repeat, louder.

He stops at the door of the bedroom, says over his shoulder, "We're even now."

"So this was what? A revenge jerk-me-off?" I feel that familiar anger from earlier, the one he seems to keep sparking in me, roar back to life.

"No." He smiles, then holds up his fingers, the ones he'd plunged inside of me only a few minutes ago. "Just a taste of how it could have been between us."

He turns to go. Stops. "I moved my things earlier. I'm taking the other room."

This time he doesn't look back when he leaves.

20

Sienna

When I wake up the next morning, the first thing I do is walk across to the other bedroom and knock on the door. When there's no answer I slide the door open, peer in.

Empty.

The bed ruthlessly made, suitcase neatly placed on the platform provided for it near the cupboard.

A pair of shoes next to the chair by the window.

I'd got what I wanted. Jace had moved to another bedroom.

But after last night, when I'd bared my soul to him, and then exploded in his arms...it feels like it's already too late. He already knows me better than anyone else.

Turning, I walk to the kitchen, grabbing a cup of coffee from the percolator. In a few minutes, I'm dressed in my running clothes and heading out.

By the time I clear the grounds and run into the open fields behind the hotel, the sun is already overhead.

I breathe in the smell of hay, the scent of the morning rain that lingers in the moist soil, leaves crunching underneath. So different from the images that often overwhelm me.

Of being surrounded by warmth. The heat in the air, sinking into my perspiration drenched skin.

A woman's laughter.

Tinkling of anklets.

Images of my birth country.

I have retrograde amnesia: the psychological impact of a tumultuous event. My adoptive parents had found me wandering in a dazed state on the streets of Bombay, half starved, drugged. Thankfully, there were no signs of abuse.

I had no identification on me. Even the clothes I'd been wearing had not been my own, so there had been no way of tracing where I came from. The Murphys had advertised locally in Bombay, even made TV appearances asking for my family to come forward, but none could conclusively prove I was theirs. And so, they adopted me.

Ma told me it was very much a case of love at first sight for her. That when she'd seen me wandering lost, chased by a group of kids, she'd stepped in and shooed them off. I'd clung to her and cried and not let go. There was no way she was leaving me behind in India.

In the months it took to process my paperwork, I settled in with them, not looking back.

I didn't miss that life.

My amnesia had wiped out all memories. My initial years in the US had been tough as I tried to fit into my new life. But I'd persevered and finally slipped into the role of an American teenager.

Had almost forgotten my earlier life.

Until five years ago.

My adoptive mother took me to an Indian temple for a wedding.

The verses were in a language which shouldn't have made sense to me, except they did. I knew then there was no escape. I could never hide from my past.

One day they'd come back and claim me.

I don't want them to. An irrational fear of losing those who I now considered my real parents made me turn my back on my Indian heritage.

That's when the dreams began. Something inside was unlocked by those chants, and now the images filtered out. Seeping into my dreams, only to disappear when I awoke.

Yet I often wake with the scent of dust and spices stuck to my skin. As if I'd walked off the crowded streets of Bombay, as if I'd been wandering through a temple. The smell of *home.*

A sense of belonging. Of feeling so right.

In Jace's arms last night, for a second, it had felt perilously close to that.

And *that* makes me stumble. I almost fall face down. Only to be hauled back and against a hard, male chest. I look up to find Eric holding me. I clutch at his sweaty T-shirt to steady myself.

He's out running too.

"I need to stop daydreaming and notice what's right in front of me sometimes." I chuckle, making to step away.

Eric's hold tightens.

I look up, into his face. His features are intense, brow furrowed, and his dark eyes sparkle down at me. They are dark enough that I can see myself reflected in them. He's still breathing hard, his chest rising and falling. But it's no longer from only the physical exertion. He's aroused. He likes me. Even as that thought dawns on me, I flush, and move away.

This time he loosens his grip on me, but still doesn't let go of my wrist.

"Eric ... " I am trying to form the words in a way that doesn't hurt him too much. He saves me from speaking.

"You don't have to do this. You don't have to sleep with him for the money."

The anger in his eyes makes me pull back from him.

Eric's trying to look out for me perhaps, though I don't know why. After all, his loyalty lies with Jace.

"He's not forcing me to do anything I don't want," I rasp.

It's true.

This may have started out as a business arrangement but it's become something else for me.

"Besides, after the stunt I pulled last night Jace is not going to hold up his end of the bargain." I laugh a little.

"You don't have to explain yourself." His voice is gentle.

This time I look beyond the brown of his eyes to see understanding, and that only makes it worse. It would have been so much easier if I had fallen for Eric.

"Well, perhaps you know something I don't, then?" I say.

"I know you did it because you wanted to get back at Jace. He took advantage of your helplessness. You saw the opportunity to hurt him and took it. Human nature is unpredictable, isn't it?" He smiles.

"Doesn't negate what I did to him. I hurt him, Eric."

I bite down on my lower lip, wondering why we are even having this conversation.

"Let me help you, Sienna." Eric lets the words hang in the air.

I know then that he'd help me pay off my debts and his proposal would be more straightforward. Nothing like the manipulative deal Jace had proposed. Eric is kindhearted, good-looking; he likes me.

He's not the man I want.

Damn.

I am well and truly sunk. I want Jace, will not settle for anyone other than him. And yet I'd gone and done the one thing that ensures there's no future together, for us.

Some of my churning emotions must have shown, for Eric opens his mouth to speak, but I cut in. "Shall we head back?"

21

———

Jace

Jace jogs into the hotel lobby. Grabbing a bottle of water from the reception desk, he runs up the wide staircase, pausing at the top to open the bottle and tilt it back, drinking from it.

A familiar laugh floats toward him.

He peers down to see Sienna walking into the lobby, followed by Eric. Both in running shorts—muddy and grass stained. They've been running through the fields.

What else have they been up to? As if what she'd done the last night wasn't enough to blow their cover, now Sienna's making sure to be seen with his friend and business partner.

As he watches, Eric leans close enough for his shoulder to brush against Sienna's.

The bottle tilts in Jace's hand, water spilling unseen, as Eric pulls at her hair. His gesture familiar.

Sienna smiles at him.

Eric puts his arm around her, and they disappear into the breakfast room.

What the—?

Jace grits his teeth and marches toward the suite.

This will not do. At all.

Sienna had committed to their arrangement and now he must make it clear that she must see the bargain through.

She doesn't have a choice.

He's going to send out a clear message to her and Eric and to the whole goddamn world that she belongs to him.

For the duration of their stay.

By the time Sienna returns, Jace has shaved, showered, and had another cup of coffee. He stands by the open window, smoking.

He doesn't look up even when she walks in and drops herself onto the large sofa, groaning a little.

"Chocolate croissants. Couldn't resist." She yawns hugely.

Pretending for all the world that she hadn't stripped last night in front of the guests and then gone off with Asher. That she hadn't spent the morning rolling in the fields with Eric.

Stubbing out the cigarette with more violence than is needed, he turns. His features are smooth, composed. No sign of the jealousy lurking inside.

His mouth goes dry.

Sienna's stretched out on the couch. Her T-shirt rides up to show a strip of skin at her waist. Smooth, soft skin. Skin that invites him to touch.

Fuck.

He can't stop following the length of her body. Over the flare of her breasts, the curve of her waist, the honeyed skin between her thighs. She crosses her legs, muscles clenching.

She too is on edge. Aroused.

When his eyes swivel to her face, it is to see her watching him with wary eyes. She's scared.

Good.

She should be.

Her tongue flicks out to lick her lips, and a curl of desire leaps to life in his belly. He plunges his hands into his jeans pockets to keep them from reaching for her.

"Seducing my friends again?" Jace snaps.

"What are you talking about?" Her cheeks flush.

"Eric," He replies, eyes still riveted by those gleaming lips, "I saw the two of you. Don't tell me you didn't come onto him. Did you ask him to help you with money too?"

She stays silent and that only maddens him further. Jealousy twists inside again, consuming him.

"And Tom." He bites out the name like it's an oath. "What's the story with him?"

"Careful, Jace, you're beginning to sound like a possessive boyfriend."

Her voice is steady, but she brings her fingers to her lips, biting her fingernails before clenching her hands at her sides.

Prowling toward where she is seated on the sofa, he bends, thrusts his face close to her. "And what if I am?"

"What?" She whispers, her voice sliding over his skin.

"Possessive."

Placing his hands on either side of her on the couch, he leans in. Knowing full well that she's effectively enclosed in the cage of his arms. Close enough for her to feel surrounded. By him.

If she can be a tease, so can he.

"Tom's a childhood friend. He had a crush on me growing up." Her voice comes out on a sigh.

His gaze slides over her lips, down her neck, toward the 'V' of her breasts. She's so petite. And beautiful.

And innocent.

He realizes with a surprise that this is why, despite all her antics from last night, he still can't stay angry with her. There's an impulsiveness to Sienna's actions he finds endearing. Despite her needing his money, she hadn't held back. She'd simply followed her heart.

"What's Tom doing here?" His eyes are drawn to her bellybutton. He wants to lick it and see if the taste there is different from her mouth.

She knows what she's doing. She's using her body to distract him.

He straightens back up, folds his arms over his chest.

Sienna cranes her neck up, the cord of her neck vulnerable. Exposing that secret hollow at the base of her throat.

The curl of heat in his belly flares. Pulling his hands out of his pockets, he folds them over his chest, looking down on her.

He will not—cannot—go to her.

"I had no idea Tom was going to be here. Honest." She widens those almond shaped eyes at him, the amber in them glinting, making her look catlike. "Surely you don't think I asked him to come...?"

Her voice is shaky. She's nervous.

Can she tell how turned on he is?

He grits his teeth trying to quell his arousal. A bead of sweat trickles down his back with the effort of standing still. Of not reaching out and hauling her to him.

She mumbles in a hoarse voice, "I'm going to take a shower."

Sienna slides off the couch, making sure not to touch him. Walks into the bedroom, leaving the door half open behind her.

Jace stands there, curling his hands into fists at his side.

She only had to look at him for him to be aroused. Surely she knew the effect she was having on him.

If not, she wouldn't have said she was going to shower. Wouldn't have left the door to the room half open so he can hear the shower running.

Don't even think about it.

The water sliding down her throat, over her breasts, in between them, down farther still between her legs, and over those smooth thighs.

Heat roars through his chest, making it difficult to breathe.

She left the door open, didn't she?

She wants Jace to come in. She'd been practically flaunting herself at him.

Don't.

And she'd agreed to this proposition? She must have known it was bound to end in this.

Of course she does.

The heat in his belly crackles into a full-fledged fire. Tearing off his T-shirt, he drops it on the ground.

Unbuttoning his jeans, he steps out of them, kicks them and his briefs out of the way. He is naked and fully aroused by the time he reaches the shower cubicle.

22

Sienna

The shower door whispers open.

Jace.

I know it's him even before his arms slide around me. He cups my breasts. His touch firm, yet gentle.

He's done this before. Knows all about a woman's body.

How will he feel about mine?

Heat spools off his chest, slamming into my back. When he moves closer, his chest muscles are firm against my back.

The curve of my butt fits into the hollow of his groin, and his arousal thrusts against me already, aggressively mimicking what he wants of me. He buries his head in my neck, licking the soft skin near my shoulders. Sliding my hair aside, he bites my nape. I'm surrounded by him, drowning in him.

A shiver runs down my back.

His hands slide down to grip my hips on either side, and he bites my neck again before licking the skin there.

I groan as a spurt of pleasure in my belly takes me by surprise. He works his way down, biting-licking-biting. Each time, my skin jumps in reaction. He reaches the curve of my butt, and his fingers dig into my pelvic bone. I wait, not daring to breathe. Wait for him to—

He kisses the skin, the touch of his lips arcing straight to my core. Desire pools between my legs.

My knees buckle, forcing me to slap my hands against the slippery tiles to hold myself up.

The heat of his chest presses against my back, and he's turning me around.

Eyes closed, I feel the flush bloom on my cheeks. I can't look at him.

Am not sure why, but a feeling of helplessness grips me.

And embarrassment.

I've been with other men. But not like this.

With Jace it's different. He sees right through me. He makes me react in ways that confuse me.

Around him I'm more unpredictable. He strips me off any pretense. Forces me to be who I am. Knowing ... knowing he'll still be there for me.

I stand there, water still beating against my back. An intense longing tugs at me.

I sense rather than see him brush his lips on mine.

Gentle.

So, gentle.

That's my undoing. Tears prick the back of my eyes.

I still can't open them, don't want to see myself reflected in his eyes.

His arms slide around me. He's all around me, over me, that pine and cloves smell now drenched in water.

My muscles tense. Not like this. I don't want to do it like this.

Oh, my body wants him all right, but not my heart when I am still trying to understand what's between us.

Even as I'm thinking that, he kisses me, nibbling on my lower lip till I open my mouth and his tongue slides in. I taste the coffee from earlier, the lingering traces of cigarette, all mixed with the deep, textured taste of him.

He lifts me up suddenly, and I cling to him, my legs wrapped around his waist, my arms around his neck. Without preamble, he slides his finger into me and I cry out against his throat.

Panic overwhelms me.

The steam in that small enclosed space is pressing in on me, forcing me further toward him. Heat from the shower, radiating off his body, from my skin. I can feel every inch of his body, as if all my nerve endings have woken up.

When he slides a second finger into me, I gasp. But I don't want to do this. Don't want to make love. Not yet.

Swearing aloud, half aroused, half mad and with a sinking feeling of helplessness that threatens to suffocate me completely, I push against him. Feel the shock ripple down his back as he loosens his arms.

My feet hit the floor with a thud.

"What?" He looks at me, eyes still clouded with desire, his arms coming to rest on my waist, holding me up so I don't slip.

The touch of his fingers on my skin once more sets my nerve cells vibrating. My eyes slide a path down his chest, following the water over his nipples, over his flat stomach toward where he's still fully aroused.

I want to ask him to leave, but can't seem to form the words. Still, my emotional struggle must have shown, for he takes his hands off me.

I brush past him, dripping water onto the bathroom floor.

23

Sienna

Slipping into my bathrobe, I wrap another towel around my wet hair with clumsy hands.

I can't trust myself to be in the same room as him right now. I walk out of my bedroom into the shared living room space.

By the time he follows me out, I'm standing in the center of the room, fingers clasped together in front of me.

Towel stretched around his hips, he stands at the door to my room, arms akimbo. He doesn't move closer and for that I am grateful.

If he touches me now, I'll give in.

And I don't want to.

Not yet.

Not when I feel as I do for him. If I sleep with him now, I'll never get over him.

I don't dare meet his eyes. Don't need to. He's livid. And still aroused.

"What was that?" he asks, his voice low and controlled. When I don't look at him, he asks again, this time the anger evident, "Are you going to tell me, or do I have to play this game of guessing how I've hurt your feelings?"

The tone in his voice says he's seen this before, done this with other women. Had the same conversation with them, and that makes me angry.

"Don't do that," I say, not even sure what I am trying to tell him. He frowns and before he can speak, I add, "Don't reduce what we have to something casual."

"You think what we did is casual?" The white of the towel blinding against his darker skin, and for the first time I see him without clothes in the light of day.

He's lean, well sculpted. The tattoo wider than I realized. It covers the upper half of his arm, swirls up over his shoulders, up one side of his throat, and then over his back.

His wet hair is slicked back from his face. Those thin lips purse, even as his eyes glisten, roving over my body.

I still feel the touch of his hands on my hips, his lips on my throat, the roughness of his jaw brushing against my back as he nibbled and kissed and—

I gasp. "I can't do this anymore."

"Can't do what, Sienna?" His voice dangerously soft.

He takes a step closer. Another. And I move back.

Till I touch the window sill. I'm standing exactly where he'd stood smoking the cigarette not more than an hour ago.

I put out both my hands, palms upwards, my face pleading for him to understand. I'm not sure what to tell him, except the feeling inside that it's not right. It's not time. Not yet.

What are you waiting for?

"Not now," I say. "I don't want to sleep with you. Yet."

He stares at me as if I've gone completely crazy, and then lets out a short laugh. "Right, well you had me fooled there, especially given you invited me in—"

"I didn't," I say, shocked. "I didn't ask you to come."

His eyebrows twist, jaw hardening.

Forcing the words out, I say, "I didn't mean to, not really."

My voice fades as I realize he's right.

I'd told him I was going to shower, left the door open. Hadn't resisted him, not in those initial minutes when he'd taken me by surprise.

You'd enjoyed it, admit it.

More than enjoyed... I'd lost myself when he'd touched me. Forgotten who I was, who he was, why I was here. Nothing else had mattered. Except his touch, his feel, his breath on my lips.

An answering tug, in my belly and—

"No."

Jace looks like he's about to lose it, but then gets ahold of himself.

"You'd do well to remember to always start what you finished. Whether in life or in business."

He turns to leave when I stop him, "And what about Darren? Does he believe our story?"

"With what you did last night, stripping in front of everyone then going with Asher to his room? No, he doesn't."

I tremble at the unleashed violence in his voice.

If I thought his trying to make love to me meant he'd forgiven me, then I was mistaken.

"But," he continues, voice soft, dangerous. "With the sparks flying between us, perhaps we can convince him that this is real. If you want your money, you need to up your game, Sienna." He flings the last sentence over his shoulder as he walks toward his bedroom.

"The way you *upped* yours?" I sneer, but my voice trembles as I say it. The double meaning of my words are not lost on him.

"If you mean that little seduction scene in there? Yeah. Just making sure the chemistry between us is convincing for when we are seen together in public again."

He leaves, shattering my heart.

24

Jace

Shedding the towel, Jace walks into the shower adjoining his own bedroom. Turning the temperature of the water to cold. All the way. The ice-cold needles tear into his skin, but he doesn't notice.

He's still hard, and all he can think of is sinking himself into her softness. Again and again.

His arousal throbs.

Not good.

He turns the force of the shower higher, wincing this time as the water pounds down on his head, his chest. Finally beating his desire into submission for now.

By the time he steps out, wrapping a towel around his waist, drying his hair with another, his head is clear.

Marginally.

When Sienna had pushed against him, asking him to release her, he'd almost growled with frustration, ready to take her right then. Hoping if he'd had her once it would be enough.

Who is he kidding?

The connection between them was deeper. He cares for her. Wants her. Wants her to want him too. If he ever thought a quick fuck was all it would take to shake his need for her, he knows now he's mistaken.

No, he wants to make love to her again and again. Drink of that heady exotic warmth that pulls at him. He wants to bury himself in her scent. That enticing vanilla and black coffee. So mysterious and seductive it drives him mad with desire to be near her. And not have her.

Fuck.

He's well and truly screwed.

Even as he thinks so, his phone buzzes.

Incoming Facetime call from Karina.

"Hey."

Karina's face appears on screen. Headpiece on, she's wearing a jacket and clearly on her way to a meeting.

"Hey, stranger, how's it going? I'm not checking up on you I promise. But the two boys were worried about you and Eric and didn't think it would be very macho if they said so. So I'm doing it instead."

Before Jace can protest that he and Eric are fine, thank you very much, she adds Damian and Arpad to the call.

"It's Karina who was worried about the two of you, I swear." Damian says, an unlit cigarette hanging from his lips. He's given up smoking but swears the unlit cigarette helps control his nicotine cravings.

"Yeah, we are here at her request." Arpad's blue silk tie is visible against a crisp white shirt.

Hearing from his friends lifts Jace's spirits. "Last I saw, Eric was trying to get in the pants of the blonde by the poolside last night."

Laughter from the other three.

"And you, Jace?" Karina asks, the sound of her heels clapping against a hard surface in the background.

He touches his thumb to his forefinger in the universal sign indicating he was fine. "I'm enjoying family time and all."

A groan from Arpad, "Sounds as enjoyable as a visit to the dentist."

"Yeah. Sounds about right," Jace grimaces.

"Blood family, man. It's important to do what it takes to keep the ties. Just like with friends," Damian adds.

"For a rocker-dude, you do often make deep sense," Karina smiles in agreement. "You and Eric have your talk yet?" This to Jace.

When Jace hesitates, Karina adds, "Yeah, I told them. Of course, they'd already guessed that things are not as serene as you claim it to be."

"We're here to help both of you," Damian drawls.

"Stop being so pigheaded and tell us when you need us to help, you obstinate fuck," Arpad growls at Jace.

Karina chuckles, "Couldn't have put it better, Moneybags."

"I got us into this trouble. I'll get us out of it," Jace says, voice serious. "But I appreciate the offer you guys. Means a lot to know you have my back."

"Always." This from Arpad

"You bet, bro," Damian adds.

"I gotta sign off. One mad film director coming up who I must bully into accepting my security measures. People don't know what's good for them, do they?" Karina mutters darkly before signing off.

The screen goes blank.

By the time he's dressed and ready to head out, Jace knows he must find a way to put things right for the business. For Eric.

And his pride will not take let him take the help from his friends. Besides, it's been grilled into him that taking money from friends is the recipe to breaking a good friendship. Another of Darren's lessons that's stuck with him.

No, Jace decides. He'll do what it takes to convince Darren about his intentions toward Sienna. By the end of this trip, the old man would willingly hand over the first part of the inheritance.

And if this means he has to tie Sienna to him in the most public of fashions, so be it.

25

Sienna

I walk down the wide staircase to the hotel lobby, where I'd told Natalie I'd meet her this morning. I head toward the door that leads to the sprawling garden outside. The space separates the main hotel from the large pool house where last night's reception had been held.

A man walks by, his arms full of fragrant flowers. He walks out the door and toward the far end of the garden where Natalie is. She directs him to place the flowers in one of the large vases next to her.

It's an outdoor wedding.

In front are rows of large pillows, set out on colorful blankets, as well as massive cushions, with little glass mirrors that catch the sun.

The entire space feels set up for a relaxed evening among friends instead of a wedding. Different from the setting last night.

"Sienna." Tom walks up to me. He hesitates, then asks, "You okay?"

I flush, knowing he's referring to my rather spectacular exit with Asher last night.

"Why wouldn't I be?" I snap, then bite my lips, "Didn't mean to yell at you."

"No offense taken, Sen," he smiles.

His calling me by my childhood name makes me feel worse. It also reminds me that he is one of my oldest friends. That I am nothing like the girl I was when he knew me then.

I look past him to where Natalie is in the distance talking to the wedding planner.

"Gorgeous, isn't she?" Tom follows my gaze. "We met at our internship in a London law firm. She didn't last a week." He grins a little. "Threw a fit when one of the partners laid a hand on her ass, slapped him and walked out."

"You saw the internship through, didn't you?" I ask.

Tom had been as keen as me to get out of Gainesville. He'd wanted to earn enough money and fast. For Tom that meant becoming a lawyer.

"We need to talk, Sienna." His serious tone makes me look up at him curious.

"Now? I'm waiting for Natalie and—"

The pleading look in his eyes bringing me up short. He jerks his head, and I follow him to a couch set in the far corner of the hotel lobby.

Behind us is a big bay window through which the wedding preparations continue.

"I need money," he says without preamble.

I look at him startled, my mind already racing forward.

His features twist as he speaks fast. He's trying to get the words out before he can change his mind. "Look, I wouldn't be doing this if I wasn't desperate."

His eyes slide away, and he clasps his hands in front of him.

"I'd help but it's not like I am rolling in money myself," I say, my tone half joking, half sarcastic.

He gives me a strange look, frowns. "You're going to be wedded to money soon. I'm sure it'll be very easy for you to loan me half a million dollars—"

"Hey," I interrupt. "I'm not officially engaged to him. And just because I'm the woman Jace happens to be sleeping with at the moment doesn't mean I have access to that kind of money," I mutter.

Natalie's laugh floats through the window. Happy, carefree. I'd do anything to feel that way again, even for one day.

"Why don't you ask Natalie? She's part of the family and has more access to the money."

When he raises his eyebrows at me, I realize he's already thought about that.

"Well?" I ask impatient. "What did she say."

"She doesn't inherit anything. All the money goes to the first male heir of the family."

"Jace," we chorus as one.

"Perhaps you should ask Jace. He may cut you a deal," I say only half serious.

"He already hates me, Sen. Since he saw me talking to you. He's jealous. He's in love with you."

"Yeah, right," I snort in disbelief. "I promise you there's nothing like that between us."

"Don't lie." He leans forward, grips my arm so tight, I yelp in pain.

"You're hurting me." I try to pull away but he doesn't let go.

The glint in his eyes has me leaning back.

"You see, Sienna, unlike Natalie, you have no choice but to help me out." His voice flat, cold, yet it wobbles as if he's trying to keep his emotions out of it and not quite succeeding.

"What do you mean?" A shiver or apprehension runs down my back. I already know I don't want to hear what he's going to say next.

"I have the video," he says.

"What are you talking about?" I ask.

My heart thuds in my chest. Whatever it is he's going to show me, I know, it can't be good.

Tom pulls out his phone, scrolls to a screen, then hands it to me. What I see on the screen makes my head whirl.

26

Sienna

I'd been eighteen and about to leave for university. Tom and I had been on a few dates together, but it had never developed further. Not for my lack of trying either. I couldn't get past the 'friend' stage with Tom.

We never had that kind of chemistry.

The last time Tom and I met, I'd been going to tell him so. Break off any hopes he'd been holding out for me. That's when he'd claimed he loved me and would miss me. Begged to kiss me.

And I had let him—but things got out of hand. Tom had pleaded with me to sleep with him, but I'd turned him down.

What I didn't know is that he'd filmed that entire encounter.

"Why?" I grip the phone, the skin stretched white over my knuckles, unable to tear my eyes from the screen. A morbid fascination has me watching the video.

Reliving the moments when we'd kissed. Passionately. And I'd tried to respond. Initially. Trying to feel something for the person who had been my best friend. Hoping for a flare of chemistry that would help me reciprocate what he felt for me.

I'd gone so far as to take off my shirt and bra. And we'd kissed again. Till his hand clamped on my breast and I'd panicked. Slapped his hand away. Right then, I'd taken a step back and told him to back off.

The video only shows the first part.

He takes the phone from my nerveless fingers, pockets it.

"I told you the truth then, Sienna. I was in love with you. Perhaps I still am," his voice is serious. "Thought I'd never see you again. This was my way of remembering you."

"And now you're going to use it to blackmail me?" I snap.

"I'm not blackmailing you," he protests.

"Sure you are. You want the money, you hold the video against me, and if I refuse to pay you, what, you release it? Go ahead, see if I care." I call his bluff, my voice firm. Inside I'm quaking, praying he'll back off.

Knowing he won't.

"I can do worse," he says. "Release it to the tabloids."

"You wouldn't," I whisper.

Fear crawls up my spine.

My pulse speeds up. Realizing I'm chewing my fingernails, I hastily drop my arm, curl my fingers into the palm of my hand.

"A video of the girlfriend of the Walker family scion making out with an old boyfriend, naked breasts on display? The tabloids would have a field day."

"All it shows is us kissing. It's not interesting enough for the newspapers." I bluster. But know he's right. There's enough there to damage me.

Jace had specifically asked that I keep our involvement out of the media. And now Tom's threatening to make this video public, to do the one thing I'd promised not to.

He'd also warned me to up my game, to do everything possible to show I am committed to our relationship. If Tom goes to the tabloids the deal is off, no chance of redemption this time.

As for the money already received from Jace? That's for Bella and to pay the salaries of my start-up team. I am not letting Tom touch that. Just thinking of it makes me angry.

"No," I say.

"What?" Tom asks.

Phone in one hand, with the other he grips my shoulder.

"If this were to come out, Jace would drop you." Tom warns. "That's the last you'll see of your 'fiancé'."

A flare of anger, and I clench my fists.

I am not going to be blackmailed into parting with the money.

And if the video does comes out, well then, it's a real test of how strong the 'relationship' is between me and Jace, isn't it?

Mind made up, I get to my feet.

"You heard me," I say, my voice firm. "No. Do whatever you want, but stay away from me."

"You'll regret it, Sen." Getting to his feet, Tom stomps off toward the staircase and the rooms.

I sit on the couch for a few seconds more, my heart twisting with the knowledge that I'd lost a friend.

One of my closest friends from my childhood days and he's let me down. I can't get my head around it.

Is this what life does to you? Change friends to foes along the way?

Sometimes enemies can surprise you and turn out to be your best friends too.

Will Jace come through for me, if this video ever comes out?

27

Sienna

After Tom leaves, I walk to the wide French doors of the hotel lobby flung open to the garden.

Spotting me, Natalie waves.

Stepping out onto the wide patio I don't have to wait very long before she bounces up the garden path toward me.

It's difficult to be in anything other than a good mood with a bride who's obviously radiant and so in love and looking forward to being married. None of the nerves or stress or fussing over last minute details or about her dress or her looks.

Stepping onto the patio she asks "Like it?"

I take in the arrangements behind her, "I love it." I say, my voice sincere.

Her eyes dart over my shoulder, "Darren," she exclaims and I stiffen.

"How does it feel to face your last day of freedom?" Darren's talking to Natalie, but I sense his eyes boring into my back.

"It might surprise you, but I actually want to marry my fiancé." She grins at him. "Unlike you, I actually intend to stay married. Once is sufficient for me."

I almost choke, but to my surprise, Darren chuckles, sounding a lot like his son. Darren loves Natalie like a daughter. But not enough to leave her a part of his inheritance.

"Touché, my dear." He holds up both his palms, signaling a truce. "You always put me in my place."

Reaching us, he bends down and kisses her cheek.

So Darren is capable of being affectionate too. Just not with Jace.

Stepping back from Darren, Natalie turns to me, "Now you know where Jace gets his charm from."

Both of them look at me. Natalie's eyes shine with mischief.

Darren's are steelier, almost slate colored with a tinge of green at the edges. So similar to Jace's. Yet different. Where Darren's are cold, Jace's eyes are more tumultuous, open.

As if Darren's the harsher, cruel side and Jace the more empathetic one.

Not that Jace would appreciate being described that way, but meeting his father brings home how genuine Jace is. Sure, he'd manipulated me, loved to control me, too—but he's been upfront about it all along.

The banquet manager calls out to her from inside the hotel. Before I can protest, she's excused herself, promising to be back in a few minutes.

I'm left standing alone with a man who I have no wish to be with.

Before I can make an excuse and leave, he reaches out to me, linking his arm through mine, in a gesture meant to be paternal.

With reluctance, I follow Darren to the other side of the grounds. The hotel is hidden by the tall hedges.

We're quite alone, and it doesn't reassure me.

I tug my arm from his and, to my relief, he lets go. But he doesn't step aside. Instead, he folds his arms over his chest and balances himself on legs slightly spread out to hold up his weight

He's fit for his age, wears his power like he's earned it. An almost magnetic appeal vibrates off him, and I take a step back to put distance between us.

A gesture not lost on him.

"Do I scare you, little girl?" His condescending tone sets me on edge.

"No," I say.

Not bothering to rise to the 'little girl' insult.

Any emotion I reveal will be construed as weakness—or worse, be used against me.

I must not show how much he affects me. For he's familiar, the flavor of the energy rippling off him reminds me of Jace. An older, more mature Jace, a more cynical one. Someone deeper, darker, with more secrets to hide.

I meet his gaze head on, refusing to blink or look away. Stay quiet. Wait for him to speak first.

Wait.

When Darren does speak, I heave a sigh of relief at winning this minor battle.

"No. You're not scared," he concedes, and his features shift. He's studied me and come to some conclusion.

"You're young in years, yet street smart," Darren's arm snakes out, latching onto my wrist.

I jump.

"How much is he paying you?" He asks.

I frown. "What do you mean?"

"Cut the bullshit," Darren's hold tightens.

Pain shoots through me, but I bite my tongue, stop myself from exclaiming aloud. Instead digging my feet into the ground, I force my muscles to relax.

"I have no idea what you're talking about," I say, pleased my voice comes out cold, flat.

"You're not Jace's girlfriend." He says without preamble.

My throat closes. I swallow the sickness that threatens to rise before saying. "You sound very confident about that."

I keep my tone light, but my heart is thumping with fear.

"Oh, I am." He barks a laugh. "You're too intelligent. Hell, you actually have a personality. Not the type he normally likes to fuck."

I cringe at the bald statement.

"Jace is paying you to put up a front, to convince me that he's changed, ready to come back to the fold. He made a mistake bringing you here. He's trying too hard and that gives him away."

My mind races ahead. Of course, he's right. That is exactly why Jace wanted me along. And yeah, I'm so not his type.

Darren watches me. Waiting for me to give myself away.

Pulling my wrist from his hold, I shake back my hair. Placing my hand on my hip, I put on a swagger, show he doesn't intimidate me. "And did it work? Have we convinced you?"

He's quiet for a second, eyebrows drawing down over his eyes. Then he laughs, a short but appreciative sound.

His eyes sweep over my face. The authority in that look makes me catch my breath. Sweat breaks out over my upper lip, and I resist the urge to wipe it off.

I am not nervous.

I refuse to be.

This time when he grips my forearm, I don't balk. "Let go of me," I say, my voice sharp.

And to my surprise he does.

Whew.

He holds my gaze though, a twist of his lips as he says, "I hope he's worth it, my dear," his voice is soft, steely. "You have a few more days to show me this relationship is authentic. You do realize that's why he brought you here. To convince me not to disinherit him. Jace took a risk, putting his future in your hands. Will you live up to his expectations, I wonder?"

Blood thunders in my veins, I fold my arms across my chest.

What? So, this entire charade has to do with Jace trying to make sure he isn't disinherited.

Doesn't surprise me, that his motive is money. After all, that's why I'm here too.

For the money.

Except it's not true. Not anymore. Somewhere along the way things changed. For me. As the knowledge dawns, I want to turn and run.

But I will not. Not now, not like this. I'd let Jace down once in front of his family. Not again. Not this time.

How dare Darren insult Jace and assume the status of our relationship.

As Darren brushes past me, I say, "Can't stomach seeing your son happy? Jealous of him, are you?"

Jace was right. His father *does* hate him.

But it's not because Jace takes for granted the kind of material comforts that his father could only dream of having when he was growing up.

No, Darren is jealous of Jace's youth. Angry that whatever he does, he'll never be able to cheat time.

"You want to be Jace, don't you?"

Darren swivels around so quickly that my heart leaps in my chest.

Adrenaline pumps through me. *Is he going to hit me?*

"Careful what you say." Fury flares in his eyes. "You may be smart, but can you see this relationship through? Make it to the altar first and then we can complete our little chat."

I know then nothing I say or do will convince him. Not unless Jace and I marry. For real. And *that* is not going to happen.

Have I lost already? Should I even stay on? Or just leave.

28

Sienna

Natalie bounds back toward us, oblivious to the tension in the air. Linking her arm through mine, she waves Darren away.

"Thanks for keeping her company, but you can leave now."

"She's all yours." Half bowing to us, Darren leaves.

The tension between my shoulders slides off, leaving me limp. I lean on Natalie, and she puts her arm around my waist, looking down at me.

"You all right?" she asks, her voice concerned.

"Yeah." I nod. "You sure you still want to hang out with me this morning?"

"You bet," she says. "Besides, when else am I going to get a chance to get to know more about Jace's mysterious girlfriend?"

"You mean the one who 'suddenly' appears on the scene, someone very different from everyone else he's brought in the past?" I smirk, echoing Darren's words.

"Very different," she agrees. "Beautiful, and not only on the outside."

"You still think so, even after last night?" I flush at the knowing look in her eyes. No doubt my little 'incident' was the main topic of discussion around the breakfast table.

"*Especially* after last night." She grins, no shock on her face.

I peer into her eyes. *Wow. She's not joking.*

"So you *don't* think I'm unfit for the 'scion' of the Walker family?" I punctuate my words with air quotes.

She laughs at that, "About time someone put Jace in his place."

"Yeah, right," I mutter in disbelief.

"No, really," she grips my arm, all mirth dropping away from her face.

"You're good for him. You stand up to him, and that's what he needs. Someone not afraid of his power, and who isn't after his money."

If only she knew.

Natalie continues, unaware of the conflict swirling inside me. "I hope Jace holds onto you." She says.

"He didn't take very kindly to my antics," I clear my throat. "If you'd seen him last night ..." my voice fades.

To my surprise, I find tears pricking my eyes. I'm not over the incident either. And I do regret my actions. But I'm unsure now how to make amends.

"Hang in there." Natalie says. "Jace can be quite macho, and overbearing. But inside he's the real deal. Honest." Voice earnest she takes both my palms between her own. "Jace has been through a lot growing up. You've met Darren, he's not an easy father. And all this" she waves around her, "growing up with this kind of money has only made it more difficult for Jace to find himself. Who he really is. That is why he needs you. You are the first genuine person in his life. You are good for him, Sienna."

I blink at the seriousness in her tone.

Her honest concern for Jace is my undoing. I want to tell her right then, that everything between me and Jace is a sham. But seeing the hope shining in her eyes, I can't bring myself to speak.

Perhaps I want to believe there's still hope for Jace and me?

Foolish.

When I don't react to her words, she says, "Well no. That wasn't all true. You are the second genuine person Jace has in his life."

"What?" I burst out.

"I am the other first." She giggles. "Gotcha."

Damn. My heart, which had begun pumping wildly, slows down. Tugging my hand out of hers, I rub it over my chest. "You. Gave. Me. A. Heart attack.."

A knowing look flares in her eyes. I've given myself away. Shown that I do have feelings for Jace.

"Let's get some lunch. Come on." She tugs me along.

We walk back into the hotel lobby, when Jace enters from the other side.

I freeze, take a step back, but Natalie grabs my arm, stopping me. I look at her, a plea on my lips. She shakes her head, a slight twinkle in her eyes as if amused by my reaction.

"You really don't want him seeing me right now," I hiss at her.

"*I really do,*" she hisses right back.

Jace stalks toward us.

His tailored pants are molded to his thighs, long-sleeved shirt showing off the column of his throat. His hair is still wet from the shower, curling at the edges as it dries. He hasn't shaved, and his chin is shadowed, lending him a dangerous look.

I want to reach out, rub my cheek against his stubble. It would be rough, prickly against my sensitive skin. Arousing. A curl of heat unfurls at the base of my belly.

His eyes lock onto mine. The silver in them glows before his eyelids sweep down. When he raises them to me next, they are blank. But he doesn't look away. He looks purposeful. He's here to get something.

"I was taking Sienna to lunch." Natalie pipes up, her voice deliberately light, provocative, "You joining us?"

That's the last thing I want. I'm not yet ready to speak with Jace.

His scent still clings to my skin, his touch on me, in me, like he was making love to me a few seconds ago. If I sit at the same table as him, next to him, I won't be able to hide how he's affecting me.

I tug my hand, but Natalie refuses to let go.

I can't pull away without making a scene either.

Damn.

I stand there helpless, shifting from foot to foot, under his scrutiny. The silence stretches.

The sound of a lawnmower starting up punches through the air and I flinch. I can't take it anymore.

"Look, there's no need to pretend anymore, is there, Jace?" I force out the words through lips gone dry.

"Pretend?" He asks, voice casual.

"This," I point to the space between us, "whatever is happening between us. I don't think we need to keep up this charade anymore."

Next to me, Natalie inhales a deep breath.

I raise my eyes to his. Don't bother hiding my emotions. Anger, confusion, regret...I let it all show. I try to tell him, without saying it aloud, that I'm sorry for what I did. That I didn't mean to hurt him. That I hadn't known what was at stake for him. That I also...care for him. I'm half in love with him.

His jaw hardens, eyes narrowing. He's made a decision. I know what's coming next. I look away, fighting the conflict of emotions inside.

"Yes," he agrees, voice grim. "No more pretense."

My throat closes at that. I half nod, not surprised. Not trusting myself to speak. When I pull away from Natalie, she doesn't hold me back. Lets me go. That sends another spurt of grief through me. The iron band around my chest tightens. It's over. Really over.

When Jace takes a step toward me, I flinch. Natalie inserts herself between us. "Let's not be hasty, cousin." Her voice is wary.

She's trying to shield me from Jace. If I liked her earlier, I am positively in love with Jace's cousin now.

He places his hands on her shoulders. "Trust me to do the right thing," he tells her, but he hasn't taken his eyes off me.

She moves aside and I swallow. "So this is, goodbye?" My voice comes out thready, my blood thudding in my ears.

"This is it," he agrees.

Sweat trickles down my back and I am sure I'm going to faint. Swallowing down the sickness, I raise my palm for a goodbye handshake.

"Wrong hand."

"What?" I blink.

Then all the breath goes out of me.

Grasping my left hand, Jace slides a ring onto my finger.

29

———————

Sienna

What the—?

He didn't just do that, did he?

Natalie yelps in delight, but I don't notice. I simply stand there, unmoving as I look from Jace to the ring on my finger.

The world tilts back into focus. And I'm well and truly pissed off at him.

Seriously?

He leads me on, letting me think we are going to break up, knowing I am getting more upset by the moment. And then...he puts a ring on my finger.

He. Didn't. Ask. Me.

I snarl, "What are you playing at? If you think—?"

He closes the distance between us. Covers my lips with his and absorbs the rest of the words. Eyes wide open in shock, I look straight into his, watching the green in them turn stormy.

Then the sweetness of his lips fills my mouth, and my eyelids shutter down. It's different, this kiss. Gentle. Not like the last few times when he'd tried to possess me. He licks his tongue over my lips, seducing, coaxing.

Asking.

And that is my undoing.

I groan in my throat, open my lips, and his tongue slips in.

Heat plumes off him, curling around me, locking me to him in a way that is unbearably familiar. Desire flares. It's as if he's absorbing the fire inside me, using it to fuel the heat in his body, his arousal throbbing against the curve of my waist.

Then, my mouth is free. So suddenly that my knees buckle. I'd have fallen if it were not for Jace holding me up. He turns me around so I stand in front of him. One of his arms wrapped around my waist, a steel band. A warning in his possessive hold, to stay silent. The other holding my left hand.

Natalie looks from me to him, a wicked smile on her face. My cheeks redden.

A smattering of claps sound from the hotel staff who've been watching us with interest.

No doubt everyone is taken in by his demonstration. Hell, I'd be taken in by it, too. For those few seconds, that slow, sweet seduction had been my undoing. But it's all a front. A public demonstration that the 'romance' is very much on. And he'd made it official.

My fingers curl around the foreign weight on my fingers. The band around my chest tightens.

Oh! How I hate being played.

30

Sienna

I stand silent in the circle of Jace's arms, while Natalie kisses me on my cheek. She flings her arms around both of us. Squeezes. Before stepping back.

"Guess that's our afternoon plans done then." She cries, voice ringing with delight. "I'm so happy for you Jace, you take good care of her now, you hear?"

Yeah right.

Behind me, Jace's muscles stiffen. "I know a good woman when I see one."

I want to elbow him in the groin. Instead, I content myself with digging my nails into the arm around my waist. Dig in with enough force, that I know it must hurt. But he doesn't flinch.

Annoying, macho man!

Blowing us a last kiss, Natalie flounces away.

I turn to him, mouth open, only to have his lips swoop down on mine again. A hard kiss. This one leaves me breathless.

"Don't spoil it now." Jace growls in a low voice. "Save it for when we're back in our suite."

Pulling me against him, so there's no mistaking his desire throbbing against my waist, he lowers his lips. Thrusting his tongue inside my mouth. A third kiss that zooms straight to my knees, leaving them weak.

Damn him!

My fingers clutch at his shirt, helpless. He has me writing in a whirlwind of anticipation.

Then he pulls me along.

Arm slung around my shoulders in a gesture meant to look possessive but which leaves me effectively imprisoned.

A slow shiver of desire, of anger twines around me.

What. The. Hell.

He's manipulating me again, this time using his sexual pull.

Fuming, I force myself to move as Jace accepts congratulations from the hotel staff.

The nerve!

As we walk through the lobby, another couple walks down. The man nodding to Jace as the woman surveys me with frankly curious eyes.

An imp of mischief makes me turn my body into Jace, melting into him. Sliding my arm around his waist, I thrust my breasts flush against his side. Leaning up on tip toe to bite on his earlobe.

And am rewarded by a shudder that runs through him. His arm around my shoulders tightens and then I'm pulled along in double quick time.

As we near the short flight of steps leading to our room, Eric walks toward us.

I stiffen, wondering if I should ask him for help.

As if sensing my intent, Jace leans down—without slowing his steps—and says in a low voice, "Don't even think about it."

"You threatening me?" I bite out the words.

"If that's how you want to interpret it." He shrugs.

His voice is mildly condescending, uncaring, and that finally pushes me over the edge.

I dig my heels in at the base of the staircase and come to a stop. Short of dragging or carrying me, Jace has no option but to listen to me now.

Eric stops in front of us and to my surprise, Jace half moves in front of me, as if trying to hide me from Eric.

"What are you doing?" I hiss at him.

In reply, he grips my waist, pulls me to him with one arm, the other on my shoulder, so I am standing on tip toe, back arched, hair falling down my back and over his hand.

"Holding my fiancé," he says, his features expressionless.

"That was a cheap trick you pulled," I say, "Giving me the ring in front of everyone."

"Not a trick," he says, voice short.

"So the ring means something?"

His eyebrows slash down, I know I've taken him by surprise.

Jace hesitates, before tilting his head. His eyes soften, as he brushes the hair from my cheek.

He feels something for me.

He does.

Before he can reply, Eric stops next to us, "I hear congratulations are in order?"

When my gaze swivels to him, he says, "Natalie told me."

"So a double celebration tonight?" He pats Jace on his shoulder.

"Tonight?" I ask.

"The stag party," Eric says. "Hasn't your fiancé told you?"

Before I can reply, the concierge hails us, "Phone call for you."

All three of us turn, and he clarifies, "Call for Ms. Sienna Murphy."

"For me?" I ask, surprised.

A puzzled look on Jace's face, which fades to disbelief, then anger.

"I didn't tell anyone I was here," I rush to clarify. "I have no idea who that is."

The silver in his eyes flares. He thinks I'm lying.

Pulling his arms from around me, he steps aside. I feel bereft, shiver as goose bumps erupt over my arms.

Jace strides away, up the staircase toward the suite.

I should be relieved that he let me go. After all, I don't care what he thinks about me, right?

I take a step up, wanting to follow him, to ask him what he'd been about to say before we were interrupted, only to have the concierge call out again.

"It seems to be urgent," he says, "It's from Bombay."

Bombay? Who's calling me from Bombay? I don't know anyone there. Not unless you count the people I knew before I lost my memory, before my American parents found me.

When I hesitate, he adds unnecessarily, "From India."

A shiver runs down my spine, and the hair on my forearms stand on end. Fear grips my heart. I don't want to take the call.

But I know I must.

I have to find out who's on the other end.

I take a step, almost stumble.

Eric steadies me, but I brush off his helping hand. I can't take my eyes off the phone the concierge is holding out. Walking toward it, I take it, holding it to my ear as if it's about to bite me any minute.

As I listen to the voice on the other end, I know my life is going to change forever.

I need to leave for Bombay on the next available flight.

31

Jace

Later that than evening, returning from the stag party, Jace walks up the garden path leading to the hotel. Stumbling over the uneven ground he sprawls. Face down. For a second, he lies there groaning, his arms spread out, hugging the paved stones. Then, the sound of footsteps grows closer, and he's being rolled over.

Eric's anxious face looms over him. "You okay?"

When Jace doesn't reply, Eric hauls him up to his feet, supporting him with an arm around his shoulders. Jace leans on Eric, who staggers under his weight.

The world swims around Jace, and he groans aloud. "Fuck."

"Yeah. Should have thought of that before you chugged down most of that bottle of whiskey," Eric replies, amused.

"Whiskey?" Jace sounds befuddled.

"You didn't even taste it, did you?" Eric says his voice angry yet controlled. "Glugged it down like it was going out of style. It was single malt. Thirty years aged," he says in an exaggeratedly sad tone. "What a waste."

"There'll be more." Jace shrugs, his tone careless.

He stumbles, almost falls again as Eric flings off his arm from around his shoulder. He stands facing Jace, arms clenched at his side.

Jace looks at him curiously. What had set Eric off now?

Jace sways a little on his feet and reaches out to clutch at Eric again.

Eric moves out of his grasp.

"So easy for you to say that." Eric's voice is tight. "Easy come, easy go. Isn't that what you believe in, Jace?"

Something in Eric's eyes makes Jace take a step back, but he's not fast enough. Eric catches him with a swing to his face that has Jace's head snapping back.

"Fuck." Jace gasps aloud. The shock from the hit ripples down his back and sets off an immediate pounding behind his eyes. Before Jace can recover, Eric punches him in the side.

Jace bends over, the breath whooshing out of him.

Eric swings again, grabs Jace around the neck.

"What the fuck's wrong with you?" Jace snarls.

Eric doesn't reply. Just squeezes the arm clamped around Jace's neck.

A burst of adrenaline has Jace shoving his elbow into Eric's stomach. He puts enough force behind the blow that Eric's grip loosens. Sliding out of Eric's grasp, Jace takes a step back, putting distance between them.

"What was that about?" Jace asks, voice strained.

Eric turns around, running his hand through his hair. He features twist slightly, as if on the verge of saying something.

"You know, I quite like what I saw just now. A man who cared about something enough to lose control," Jace says, and Eric stiffens.

"Don't give me your warped, pop philosophy," Eric bites back.

Jace frowns. "I mean it. Though I still don't understand what brought that on."

"It's all a lark for you." Eric stands straight, arms folded over his chest. "The money needed for the business, the proposition to Sienna, being engaged to her."

Jace's anger flares. "I told you I'll get the money," he snaps. "And Sienna being here is definitely going to make an impact. She's an adult, knows what she's doing. She knows the engagement is a necessary prop. It gets everyone believing the story. Besides," Jace looks at Eric, forehead furrowed, "why are you so worried about her?"

Drunk and struggling to focus, Jace notices the angry twist to Eric's features.

"You've fallen for her," Jace says.

Eric winces, but doesn't deny it. "It doesn't make a damn difference what I feel. What matters is that—"

"Of course it does." Jace snaps. "You want her? Then fight for her." He holds up his hands, curled into fists, and takes a fighter's stance.

When Eric hesitates, Jace prods him, "Come on, Eric. Be a man."

"I've seen the way you look at her. Don't deny that you want her." Eric shoots back.

Jace goes still. "Don't go there, Eric," he warns.

"When are you going to tell her?" Eric asks, as if he hasn't heard Jace at all.

"You are the last person I'm going to discussing this with," Jace says.

"You're right. I'm not fighting you over this, Jace."

"Oh, yeah?" Jace sneers.

"Yeah. I'm leaving your company."

"What?" Jace asks, not sure what Eric means. Hands held up, he bounces on his feet, in a fighter's stance. "We were always partners, anyway"

"No, we're not, and you know that. I was your employee. It's your company, and you can do as you please now. I'm done here." Eric turns and walks past him, back the way they'd come.

About to call his friend back, Jace stops. It's obvious: Eric's crushing on Sienna.

Continuing toward the hotel, a spurt of jealousy tightens Jace's gut. He's jealous about Eric's depth of feeling. He's also strangely relieved to see him go.

Sure, he's going to miss Eric, but if this is how his friend feels about Sienna—if Eric likes her enough to break up with his business partner of the last five years—then it's best Eric leaves now.

And Sienna? How does she feel about Eric?

He's not going to tolerate her having any feelings for Eric or for any other man. Not as long as she's his fiancé. Sure, it's a pretend relationship, but she belongs to him for the next few days. And he's going to make sure she thinks of no one except him during that time.

32

Sienna

I've booked my flight to Bombay. My bags are packed. I'd hoped to leave without meeting Jace again. Just sidle out without warning, being the coward that I am.

No such luck.

One minute I'm asleep, and the next I shoot upright, my heart hammering in my ears.

Then I hear it: someone pounding on the door to my bedroom. I'd locked the door to my room to make sure Jace couldn't come in.

"Sienna."

Jace's voice is loud enough to make me start.

"Open the door. I know you're in there."

I don't move.

Jace pounds on the door again.

"Goddammit woman," he roars. "Open. The. Damn. Door!"

Before he's completed the statement, I'm on my feet and at the door. I fling it open.

Jace's hand is poised to bang on the door again, the other thrust up against the door frame for support. He stands motionless, silver-green eyes wide and more opaque than usual.

His jacket is muddy, his tie half off. I wince on seeing the cut on his upper cheek.

All of which, of course, only makes him look even more appealing. A slow tug pulls at the base of my stomach. I take a deep breath to squash down that melting feeling.

"You're biting your nails," he says, voice husky.

"What?" I start guiltily.

Dropping my hand to my side, my fingers curl into a fist. *I'm still wearing his ring.* I shove my hand behind my back.

He brushes past me, holding himself stiff. Movements controlled. Jace takes one heavy step, and another.

The sharp reek of alcohol hits me.

He's drunk out of his skull. Even as I think that, he trips over the carpet and goes sprawling.

What the—?

I leap toward him and sink to my knees next to his fallen body.

"Dammit. Did you hurt yourself?" I ask, my hands hovering over him.

When he doesn't move, I begin to fret in earnest. It's not like Jace to be so docile, so submissive. Unless...he's injured.

Worry twists my gut. Gripping his shoulders, I urge him to turn. When he's on his back, I lean back on my heels and stare down. His eyes are still closed and his arms stretched out. The smell of alcohol hits me afresh.

"Did you roll around in a pool of booze?" My voice comes out sharper than I intended.

"Stag night," he says, his voice hoarse.

He swallows, and I notice the redness around his throat.

"You get into a fight as well?"

His eyes flutter open, barely enough for a gleam of silver to shine through. "Yeah."

His fingers creep up my bare thigh. I slap at his bruised knuckles.

"Who did you fight with? The bar staff?"

A guilty look steals up his face. He looks young, vulnerable. Reaching out, I brush the hair off his forehead.

"Eric?" I ask.

He goes still, his eyes slide away.

Lucky guess.

"Seriously?" I blow out a breath, "You've been brawling with your business partner?"

"Ex-business partner," he mumbles.

"You guys fought and broke up? What, are you five?" I ask in an impatient voice. "Now you're going to ask Mommy to kiss the wounds better. That's why you're here, right?"

As soon as the words are out, I want to take them back. But it's too late.

His eyebrows shoot up. It's the excuse he was waiting for.

"Will you?" His hands once more creep up the flesh of my thigh exposed by my shorts.

I gasp, try to back away.

But he grips my leg, squeezing the soft flesh.

A sliver of pleasure crawls toward my center. I shiver. My heartbeat goes up a notch.

When I try to edge away, his other arm winds around my waist.

"Kiss me." He pulls my head down.

His fingers brush the edge of my shorts. Sneak under it.

My lips are so close I can smell his breath. His alcohol-laced breath. I cough, pull back.

"Brush your teeth first," I gasp.

He looks stunned. The expression on his face is so comical, I chuckle.

"I'll help you up." Gripping his hand—the one still on my thigh—I get to my feet, heaving him up.

He doesn't protest.

Using my shoulder as leverage, he tries to get to his feet. Stumbles. I fling my arm around his waist and together we teeter to a standing position.

Jace leans his weight on me. Panting a little, I walk toward the bathroom, half-dragging him along.

Leaving him to rinse out his mouth, I go out to get a glass of water. By the time I come back to the bedroom, he's stretched out on the sheets, fast asleep.

I place the glass of water on the side table next to him.

In sleep, his face is peaceful, the moonlight flowing over those high cheekbones. He looks beautiful, his face all planes and angles.

Bending down, I brush my lips over his. He doesn't stir.

A wave of fatigue washes over me, and I crawl under the covers, on the far side of the bed. *Won't harm to sleep next to him, on our last night together.*

Turning my back on Jace, I shut my eyes.

Big mistake.

A solid wall of warmth against my back, and I burrow against it. A hand snakes across my waist, pulling me closer. Heat spools over me, into my skin. Sinking in. I let the sensations wash over me.

A touch glides over my arm, leaving goose bumps in its wake. I push back against the unyielding wall of muscle at my back. His breath shudders over my neck, bringing with it that fresh sea-breeze smell. I know then where I am.

In bed.

With Jace.

And he's holding me.

I feel his hardness against the curve of my hip. He's so close, the feel of his skin surrounding me. His chest rising and falling in tandem with mine as if we were in synchrony.

Liquid desire pools in my belly, and a shudder runs down my back. I know then I must leave.

Now.

If I stay, we'll make love. I'll never get Jace out of my head after that.

But this is my last night here with him.

I hesitate, unsure what to do.

Jace makes the decision for me. He grips my hips and hauls me closer till I am pressed up against him.

His toenails scrape across the sole of my feet, and I shiver as the vibrations ripple over me.

His fingers slip under my shorts, under the lace of my panties, and a fresh wave of heat erupts inside.

Mercy.

I want him, I do. And it's not the money, or his status. It's the man himself. Who he is. The vulnerable man I'd glimpsed confused about his feelings for Asher. The one who yet misses his mother, yet portrays that tough, hardened investor to the world.

My very own fallen angel.

And I want him to want me.

I become aware of a hollow feeling deep inside. A pulse springing to life, pushing me to seek him out. The molten feeling grows, wetness pooling between my thighs. I lock my knees together, mouth going dry.

Without opening my eyes, I try to turn, only to find he's holding me in place.

That secret core inside me pulls at him, and I can smell his arousal. A deep, warm, musky scent that sends another spurt of molten heat through me.

I moan and try to turn again. As if understanding what I want, he pushes his finger inside me. I gasp and almost come with the shock.

"Shh." He blows against my ear and I shiver, even as he slides another finger inside. The heel of his hand brushes against my soft curls, tugging at me, pulling, and I moan again.

Hearing myself is so erotic, it turns me on even more. I lock my thighs around his hand, holding him captive. My muscles clench, and I try to pull him deeper inside.

His fingers dip in-out-in and I groan, bringing up my knees almost to my chest, curling around that throbbing in my center.

My fingers grip his forearm, feeling his muscles move. In and out, in and out, till it feels as if he's holding me with an invisible thread that runs all the way inside, deeper inside than I've ever let myself feel.

He turns, sliding me over so I am on top of him, my back on his chest, my thighs still wrapped around his hand. His other hand cups my breast, massaging it gently before squeezing the nipple.

The pulse throbbing inside me speeds up, slamming my heart against my chest. I pant as if I've been running for miles. Fling my arms up and around his neck. When his beard scrapes against my forearm, it only maddens me further.

He slips a third finger in, still rhythmically thrusting in and out before reaching deep inside. I arch my back as something inside me pushes through, sweeping aside the wall I've been trying to build between us from the first moment we met. Reaching, reaching, till the desire explodes out of me. I cry out as I come, the keening sound strange even to my own ears.

When I open my eyes, I'm on my back with Jace's face hovering over me. His hair is mussed, silver-green eyes narrowed. He's watching me, waiting for my reaction to what happened.

My arms are splayed out on either side. Remembering how I'd climaxed makes me flush.

His eyes widen, and the green of his irises seems to grow brighter, rising in waves till his eyes glow with an intensity that makes my mouth go dry.

My heart pounds, the pulse beating at my temples, and my breath comes in short gasps.

His gaze falls to my chest before sliding back to my face.

Silent, he touches my cheek, tucking a stray strand of hair behind my ear.

"I won't hurt you," he says.

"I know," I stutter.

"But you don't trust me," he sighs softly, his breath shuddering over my throat.

"No, I don't," I say, my voice coming out rough. "But I still want you."

His eyes widen, the silver in them clashing with the green. He's turned on by what I said.

He leans close enough for me to feel his heart thud against his chest. Or perhaps that's my heartbeat moving up a notch.

It doesn't matter. Not when he's looking at me as if I am the only thing between him and certain death.

Placing his arms on either side of me, he supports himself on his forearms. Muscles straining to hold up his weight.

"Say that again." His voice whispers over my skin.

"That again," I say, half teasing.

He leans in, pressing his erection against me, and I gasp aloud. The heat pours off him, surrounding me. Sweat breaks out over my forehead, and I grit my teeth to keep from reaching out and hauling him into me.

"Say it," his voice soft yet threatening.

"I want you—"

Before I complete my sentence, he captures my mouth.

33

Sienna

Jace kisses me, sliding his tongue into my mouth with an ease that has me shuddering. I surge up against him.

Scissoring my legs around his waist, I fling my arms around his shoulders and haul myself against him.

I bite down on his lips, drawing blood. The metallic tang fills my mouth and I break away, gasping, looking down to where a drop of blood seeps up through the broken skin.

Grasping my T-shirt, he pulls it off, throwing it aside. Before bending down and capturing my erect nipple. A pulse of light shudders through my skin.

That arouses me even more, driving me a little over the edge. Blind with desire, I lean in and bite his shoulder.

This time, I feel the shudder go through him.

Sliding to his feet, he sheds his pants. He's back again and before I can draw breath, he pulls of my shorts and my panties with it. Then he's inside me. One minute I am empty. The next, he fills me.

It's like he's possessing me.

A moan wells up, only to be swallowed by his mouth.

He's still for a second. Absorbing the sound. Drinking of my essence. Of me.

Then he angles himself, going deeper, more inside than anyone has ever been before, into that secret emotional part of me I've always held back, hidden even from myself. And when I cry out, he's already there, his mouth on mine to absorb the sound of pain and anger and something more, an emotion I can't quite understand myself.

My hand grips his hair, the other holding his upper arm, feeling his biceps flex. His shoulders clench as he pulls back, thrusts again. And again. I scream as I come, waves of pleasure travel up my spine.

Jace groans, climaxing with me. Then his body collapses on mine, pinning me to the bed. I hold him to me.

We stay there unmoving, for seconds, minutes. I feel like he's become a part of me. His muscles bunch, and I know he's going to pull away. Panic grips me.

I don't want to let go.

If I do, I know I won't let myself back.

Don't go.

I brush my lips against his. My inner muscles shiver up against him, groaning in my throat.

And then he's kissing me back.

It's a long time before we fall asleep.

By the time he opens his eyes again, I'll be gone.

34

Jace

When Jace reaches for Sienna, there's no one there. No warm skin flowing under his. His eyes fly open. That warm-honey essence of hers is still flowing through his blood and making him hard. He's erect, thirsty for her. He looks over to her side of the bed to find it empty.

"Fuck." Jace swings his feet to the floor, looks around.

Nothing.

The T-shirt and shorts that he'd torn off her last night and thrown to the floor; her cosmetics from the dressing table, all gone. So is her suitcase.

Going to the bathroom, he flings it open. He can't stop himself from hoping. Then, still naked, not bothering to get dressed, he walks across the living room space to his room on the other side.

She's. Not. There.

Walking back into the bedroom where they'd made love, he's

struck anew by the mussed-up bed, the scent of sex still in the air. And below that, her perfume that lingers.

The now familiar black coffee and vanilla. Mysterious, addictive. It still pulls at him and he's surprised to find himself harden again.

He swears at his foolishness. At his inability to hold back when it comes to her.

From the moment, the PI had sent him her pictures, he'd been attracted to Sienna. He'd wanted her even before he'd met her. Liquid fire: her essence tugged at his gut in a way that had him wanting to both shake some sense into her, yet protect her.

And when he'd gotten to know her better, that feeling had grown. Her moods, which changed by the minute, her temper often catching him unawares. He'd been unable to pin her down. And that had only challenged him to go after her.

All she had to do was unleash those sparks in her tawny eyes, and he'd be begging at her feet, ready to do whatever she wanted. He'd tried to hold back, bury what he felt deep inside in a place she couldn't get to. He'd almost succeeded in hiding the emotional part. His physical reaction had been far more difficult to disguise.

He laughs, a humorless chuckle, and runs his fingers through his hair before dropping them to his side. It'd been her secretiveness that had made him pursue her. Those unspoken secrets buried inside her. Secrets she hadn't admitted to herself. Submerged behind walls so deep she probably didn't know they existed. But he'd tasted them, those flavors of her that pulled at him.

The hint of loneliness, the vulnerability that was also her strength, made him want him to lean into her. And sometime in the last few days, he had submitted himself. Allowed himself to be taken in by the charade.

Or perhaps it was the surprise of meeting Asher after all these years that had made him weak. Reminding him again of his mother's death. And along with that, the emotional kick of meeting his father had hit him in the gut.

It had lowered his barriers. Had made him turn to her. His own solace in a world overwhelming him with emotions. His fiancé. He'd come to see her as his own.

Except she'd never been his.

Sienna is an employee, someone hired to do a job. One she hadn't completed.

Jace stares out the window. Tonight is Natalie's wedding, and Sienna wouldn't be there.

The one thing he'd asked her for, and she'd failed. She'd known he needed her there. Only a few more hours, and he would have convinced his father about his suitability for the inheritance.

As the reality of his situation dawns, anger pours through him, churning his guts.

He's going to make sure Sienna doesn't receive the rest of the money. But first, he is going to find her, and make her pay for hurting him. For leaving him the most vulnerable he'd ever been.

He starts to head out of the room, only to hesitate at the threshold. He's not even sure what he's looking for, not till he sees the table on her side of the bed. It's empty.

And the tightness in his chest fades somewhat.

She's taken the ring with her.

He doesn't question why that sends a pulse of reassurance through him.

35

Sienna

I shouldn't confuse the physical with the emotional. I've told myself that a hundred times before, and yet, as I stare out of the window of the plane, all I can relive are those moments.

A gaze.

A touch.

A kiss.

His fingers splayed out on my waist, reaching out to where the skin dips down to my core. His lips brushing mine, tongue thrusting inside. His fingers running over my skin, in me.

The heat from his body coiling around me, making me feel safe, protected, cherished.

A dream. It was all a dream. Unreal.

A business transaction, that's all it was for him. But it had become so much more for me.

If I had stayed, could I have convinced Darren that Jace was serious about settling down and starting a family? Would it have kept Darren from disinheriting Jace? I'll never know.

I am on the flight en route to Bombay. I had to leave. That call left me no choice.

Accepting the glass of wine from the stewardess, I notice the ring on my finger. *His* ring. In my hurry to leave, I'd forgotten to take it off.

Or perhaps I'd wanted to keep it a little longer. There's no doubt in my mind that I'm going to send it back to him. But for now I can still pretend I had a connection with him, right?

You'd slept with him, that's all. It's not like you are his fiancée. Or that one night meant anything to him.

Yet I'd sensed a depth of emotion from him when we made love. He couldn't have been faking it. Not all of it. He couldn't have been.

It had been real for me. Everything that I had shown him, had shared with him. As real as the ring he'd given me. Too bad Jace doesn't feel the same way.

A few hours later, as the flight begins its descent toward Bombay, I can't stop my fingers from worrying the ring. My heart pounds in my chest, the pulse beating in my ears so hard I think I'm going to faint. I force myself to breathe in and out, trying to calm myself down.

What am I even doing on this flight? One call, and I'd left Jace. broken my promise to him. All I'd needed was an excuse to leave, and I had grabbed this chance to go back in time.

Seems it's easier to face an unknown past than a future I can't see, one I can't even begin to fathom without Jace.

But now when I'm so close to finally being back—back to where it had all started—I know I've made a mistake.

By now the wedding is over and he'll be left explaining why I'm not there. And I'm going to face the one thing I have spent all my life running away from.

36

Sienna

When I step off the flight at Bombay, the heat crushes me. The moisture in the air hangs heavy, condensing inside the airport. Sweat trickles down my back. I'm jetlagged from not having slept on the flight, and the world blurs around the edges.

As I leave the airport, the noise slams into me with a physical force that almost blows me back. And the smell. That mix of mud and dirt and unwashed human bodies all overlaid with a sense of intense desperation. Of too many souls being crammed into too little a space. It echoes faint memories, flavors I've stored in that secret place inside that now come pouring out.

I don't want to be here.

But what are my options? Go back and face my debtors in the Valley? Face a furious Jace, who no doubt is even now plotting his revenge for breaking our arrangement?

No, I must keep going.

Swept along by the taxi queue, I find myself in a cab and sink back against the faux-leather seats.

The voice on the other end of the line had been frank. I had to come, immediately, to the address he had shared. Time is of the essence.

All these years, and now it's as if time has run out. Abruptly.

I'm here. And for the first time since the call, I let myself think about what lies on the other side of this journey.

My biological mother tracked me down. Found me in the one place in this world I hadn't told anyone I would be. And she's dying.

She'd spent years looking for me, trying to reach me. Ironically, it was the trip to London that had put me on their radar.

London is geographically the closest I've been to the country of my birth. Perhaps that was one of the reasons I hadn't been comfortable since I'd arrived there—a sense of my life about to change forever.

The PI, who'd been working on my case for years, had traced me to the orphanage that had helped place me, only to find all their records were lost in a fire. Still, they'd remembered I'd been placed in the US, but all other details were lost.

My mother had not given up, though. Using digitally enhanced images that aged me as I grew, the PI tried to trace me over the years, routinely tracking international flights.

The first international flight I'd taken out of the US, and he had found me.

I am not sure what to feel. My thoughts race around in my head, buzzing about, trying to make connections.

If I hadn't met Jace, hadn't accepted his offer, I wouldn't have come to London. My blood family wouldn't have found me. And I wouldn't be here, bumping along through the mid-morning traffic, eyes scrunched up behind oversized sunglasses.

I didn't want to be found.

All these years, I was hiding from them, from myself, pretending my adopted family was the only reality I knew. I'd spent years putting up those barriers. I didn't want to go back.

Didn't want to face my past.

But my gut had known. My subconscious had always been pulled here. In my weaker moments, those memories in the deepest, darkest corners of my soul had pushed through, made themselves known. Enough to let me know the life I left behind is still here.

I'd tried to turn my back on my past, but no more.

I'm here and now I have to face it.

I look out the window, my eyes glazing over with tiredness. Emotions long suppressed now pour through me, coursing through my veins, blurring my vision. Around me, the traffic ebbs and flows, as if with a life of its own.

We crawl forward. The car stops, starts, stops. Then we hit a highway and pick up speed, turning a corner from where I can see the bay of the Arabian Sea stretch out. It's fringed on this side by shanty towns and small, bobbing boats with fishermen bringing in the catch from the sea.

We hit a toll and then turn onto a sweeping bridge.

The taxi drives smoothly through the eight-lane highway. Muddy, dark-green water rolls below before giving away to a skyline of towers and soaring new buildings.

What a contrast. Like crossing from one world to the next.

I shake my head, trying to clear the thoughts buzzing around it. But I can't stop thinking of my blood mother.

All these years and now? Why now? Why call me to tell me she's dying?

Why not have let me be with Jace?

In a way, the timing of the call couldn't have been better. And if I had been waiting for a sign to get out of there, this was it.

We turn off the bridge onto a road skirting the sea and then turn in, onto a side road.

We're close now. My heart slams into my ribs, my pulse pounding in my ears as if I've been running for miles. The sweat oozes down my forehead, and my breath comes in short gasps. I think I'm going to be sick. I almost reach out to tell the cab driver to stop, but by then he's drawing up in front of a small house. It's surrounded by soaring apartment-blocks.

But this structure, time forgot.

The driver unloads my bag and opens the door. I force my legs to move. Then I'm out of the car and looking at the bungalow.

It's two stories tall, gracious, built in a colonial style. The name engraved on its side says, "Napeansea Grange - built 1918."

The walls are painted white and sparkle in the afternoon sunshine. A porch runs around the front of the house. On it, a wooden swing creaks in the light wind.

Small shrubs spread out in one corner in front of a luxurious lawn that stretches along both sides of the driveway. A clear indication that, despite the boiling heat, they are well cared for.

The overall feeling is one of quiet wealth. Dignity, and a pace of life that is gentle, unhurried, very different from the world I know. An entire continent away from Silicon Valley. It's as if I have stepped off the flight and gone back in time.

Dragging my suitcase, I walk under a tall tree shading the driveway.

Small red and yellow flowers, unlike any I have seen before, dot the ground. I focus on them, drawing strength from the colors. One step, and then another.

Then I'm at the door and ringing the bell.

When it opens, I don't look up immediately. I can't. My eyes fall on the feet of the person standing there. Big feet, male feet, clad in open-toed shoes. Pale toenails set against light-ebony skin. Skin lighter than mine, of a color that hints at mixed heritage.

Unable to stop myself, my eyes run up the faded jeans, flat waist, the dark skin visible through the threadbare cotton shirt open at the neck, curved lips turning down into a frown, and dark blue eyes.

"Sienna?" asks the handsome man in his late forties. At my nod, he holds out his hand, "I'm Neil D'Souza, your mother's friend and lawyer."

He ushers me as a servant takes my bag from me.

"Your mother's inside," he says, leading me into a spacious living room with ceiling fans that whirl up the hot air.

I seat myself on the comfortable sofa. An older man materializes bringing me a cool drink.

I sip it, and sigh in delight. It's delicious, refreshing, and a taste I can't quite get a handle on. A medley of sweet and tangy, a fusion of flavors.

"A local drink, a blend of gooseberry and herbs over crushed ice," Neil explains.

"Gooseberry?" I frown.

"It's common in these parts." He smiles.

I set down the glass on the side table and fold my hands together, then say, "Was it you on the phone?"

He nods, "I'm your mother's, Anja Deol's, lawyer," he says.

Anja Deol.

I roll it around in my head, try it out over my tongue, whisper it to myself, letting the syllables ripple over my skin. It sounds alien.

Nothing familiar about it.

I shut my eyes, try to recall those images that come to me often in the early hours of the day, when I'm suspended between sleep and being awake, but find nothing.

Nothing except loneliness, and hurt. And anger at being made to face up to a past I'm not ready for.

"Don't you want to know what name she gave you when you were born?" Neil asks.

"No," I lie, "It's irrelevant. I'm Sienna Murphy."

He looks taken aback.

"It must all be so overwhelming," he says, his voice soft, persuasive. "But first meet your mother, hear her out. She has something very important to tell you." He hesitates. "Your mother's unwell, Sienna, she's been ailing for the last year. I've been helping care for her. She doesn't have much time."

I hear him, but I'm numb, not sure what to feel. Then he's on his feet, and guiding me toward the closed door at the far end of the corridor. He knocks on it, and pushes it open without waiting for an answer.

I am not ready for this.

37

Sienna

I follow Neil into my mother's room.

The first thing that hits me is that sharp smell of antiseptic and, below that, the strong, sweet smell of something I can't quite identify.

It's cool in here, the air conditioning turned up high enough to beat even the extreme heat outside.

The room is large with high ceilings. A bookcase covers one wall. In the middle of the room is a four-poster bed, the old-fashioned kind, and in the center of it, a figure ... At least, I think the slight bump in the middle is my mother.

"She's awake, but still groggy from yesterday's chemo session," Neil explains, but I barely hear him.

He walks toward the bed, before leaning over the figure. Turning, he beckons me over.

My sneakers make soft shuffling noises as I walk across the floor. I stop by the bed, to look down at the woman covered by blankets. She's so thin she barely makes a dent.

Her eyes are open, and she's looking at me, the look in her eyes echoing what I feel. Stunned surprise. Shock. She can't believe I am here. I can't either.

Just like that, tears fill my eyes.

Seeing her so helpless—body wasted, head wrapped in a scarf, grooves running up her cheeks on a face ravaged by pain—sends a piercing ache through me.

I don't know her, don't remember her face. She's nothing like the ghosts that sometimes whisper at the fringes of my consciousness. And yet, something in her desperation pulls at me.

When she holds out her hand, I grip it and sink down on the bed next to her.

The door shuts behind Neil, but all my attention is taken up by this woman who is my blood mother.

A woman's laughter.

My mother's laughter.

Tinkling of anklets.

My mother loved to dance. Now her once beautiful form is ravaged by disease.

My mother opens her mouth but no words emerge. Her eyes dart to the glass on the nightstand. I pick it up and, helping her sit up, hold it to her lips. She leans against the headboard and gulps down the water.

When she finishes, I place the glass back and turn to her. Her eyes shimmer with tears. This time, it's me who reaches out to grip her hand, clasping it in both of mine.

In her eyes—amber eyes so like mine—I see regret, love, and below it all a spark of anger.

A ripple of emotion races through me. Hurt, anger, affection and something else. A pull of trust. Of deep, unshakeable faith. A certainty that this woman is my mother.

I just know it.

I shake my head, still unable to speak but wanting to tell her it is okay, that I am here now. That we'll figure it out. That it didn't matter what had happened in the past, to get us to this stage.

That it didn't matter how I had come to be wandering around on my own, with no memory at the age of five.

It was enough that she had found me now.

We sit there not saying anything, yet saying so much to each other.

Then Anja begins to speak. She doesn't stop. It's as if all the words, conversations she'd stored up to have with me—her long-lost daughter—all of it comes pouring out.

She tells me everything.

Anja passes away a week later. I stay with her till the end.

38

Sienna

Anja was cremated this morning, and I spread her ashes across the waves of the Arabian Sea.

Since she passed away, I've been numb. I'm not sure what I am supposed to feel. Regret at all the time I didn't have with her? Or perhaps I should be grateful that I had a week with her. Right now, I feel empty, as if all my emotions have drained away with her.

Neil and I are back at the bungalow.

So I sit in the study that had once been my father's, hands wrapped around a cup of hot tea, and wait for Neil to speak.

Books line an entire wall and on a mantelpiece sits pictures of a family. My family. One I am getting to know. Of my mother and father and me in happier times.

There are also pictures of me as a baby, as a little girl, till I'd been kidnapped at five.

Those gaps in my memory now have places and colors attached to them, but it still feels alien. As if I'm trying on a skin and finding it doesn't quite fit.

"She missed you a lot and so did your father," Neil says in that soft voice of his, drawing my attention away from the pictures.

I know my face wears the emotions I'm feeling inside. I can't put it off, not any more.

The last week has been about Anja, about spending as much time as I could with her, knowing I was going to lose her and yet trying to peer through her to see if I could glimpse the image of the mother she must have been in her younger years.

In the few days I had with my mother, she'd told me a little bit about having lost me when I was young. Now I ask Neil the inevitable questions about my past.

"You were taken," he says. "Kidnapped from school. Part of a wave of extortions taking place at that time. Your father was a powerful man. He worked for the police and was instrumental in breaking a ring of terrorists. He foiled what could have been a second 26/11 in the city."

He's referring to 2008 when terrorists had carried out a series of bombing attacks across the city. It had left many dead, and injured hundreds.

"So I was kidnapped as a way of getting back at him?"

Neil nods. "Your father refused to pay them off and your mother never forgave him for that. He was clear that he had to set an example by not bowing to their pressure. And he was confident that he would be able to track down the kidnappers, which he did—"

"But it was too late," I say, my voice soft. "I remember parts of it. Voices, images that have grown stronger in the last week. The men who took me, they kept me locked in a room for a few weeks. They..." I swallow. "They kept me drugged. So, the memories of those days are hazy. But I get flavors of what happened then, do you understand?"

"Do you remember how you escaped?"

Coming to Bombay and seeing my mother helped in at least one way. Over the last few nights some more of the memories have revealed themselves. "One of the kidnappers let me go. He told me I reminded him of his daughter. The next thing I remember is almost meeting with an accident."

Screech of vehicles—

Screams—

"My adoptive father pulling me out of the path of an oncoming car."

"I'm glad we found you in time. At least you got to spend a few days with her," Neil says.

Yeah.

Thinking about Anja is still difficult. It feels unfair that I got to meet her only to have her taken away from me so soon. My breathing goes shallow. It's difficult to draw air into my lungs, let alone speak.

"Your mother had this uncanny confidence, even after all these years, that she was going to find you." Neil's voice cuts through the emotions swirling in my head.

"Fate," he says, "can be cruel and yet sometimes we are all at its mercy. Pieces of a puzzle waiting to be put together, and the pattern that emerges always surprises."

"We ran checks on you," Neil says, his voice apologetic. "There's more," he says, his voice gentle, but with a thread of steel running through it, one I hadn't heard earlier. "Your mother left a will. She left everything to you. Your father was careful with his investments. Enough to leave your mother well taken care of. All of it, and this house, which is on some of the most expensive real estate in the world, it all goes to you."

I hear him, but my brain is still not able to process what he means by it.

"You are a very rich woman, Sienna."

I start.

My blood family is gone, but they've left me money. A lot of it, by the sounds of it.

"I don't deserve the money," I say, looking around the room again. The space is heavy with memories.

The ghosts of my parents still live here. The ghosts I have carried in my head for so long that they seem more real than the pictures on the mantelpiece.

Neil walks around the desk and sits down in the chair next to me. He grips my hand and I feel the affection, the sympathy, bleed into me from his touch.

"She'd want you to have it." he says. "They'd both have wanted you to have it."

I stay quiet, then finally ask, "My name. What is it?"

"Tara," he says. "You are Tara Deol."

I smile at that, a weight lifts off my chest. I don't recognize the name. But I like it. It sounds... "Pretty," I say.

"Your grandmother, your father's mother, was called Tara too. It means 'star'. You were the light of their lives."

I bow my head, humbled by the love and affection I feel in his voice for my family, for the little girl I was.

We stay quiet for a few more minutes. Then Neil asks, "You can use the money, can't you?"

I bark out a laugh.

The thought hadn't even crossed my mind, not till now. In everything that's happened the last week, I'd almost forgotten about what I'd left behind in the Valley. But now, with Anja gone, there's nothing left between me and the future I have to face.

"Yes," I say, an idea forming. "Yes, I can.".

I was going to use the money, and not only to pay off my debts and secure Bella's future.

But even the money doesn't prepare me for what's to come next.

39

Sienna

A month later, Silicon Valley

After leaving Bombay, I returned to Silicon Valley, determined to pay off my debts and start anew. I'd asked Neil to stay on as caretaker of the family home in Bombay, and he'd agreed. He's also the tie that binds me to my home country and I'd promised to visit again. Soon.

The first thing I'd done with my inheritance was to return Jace's loan of half a million. Had trembled even as I'd sent off the bank transfer, wondering if it would make him contact me.

But nothing.

Silence.

I'd been both relieved yet also disappointed. Had hoped he'd respond to seeing the money. That he'd track me down, come storming inside my new office, and ask me why I'd left him so suddenly.

After that incredible night together.

The feel of his skin on mine.

His fingers tracing a path down my waist, down toward my core. To where I'd felt empty since.

Stupid.

"Sienna."

Eric, Jace's ex-partner, walks into our shared office. He'd contacted me a week after my return with a proposal to work together. I'd been unsure about it at first. And not because of his connection with Jace.

But I know Eric likes me.

And yet, his suggestion of using his business acumen to help turn around my company was something I couldn't turn down.

Besides, Jace had trusted him. And that was enough for me.

Or maybe partnering with Eric was my way of holding onto a tenuous connection with Jace.

"You headed out?" He asks from across the boxes still strewn on the floor. We'd moved into this office a few weeks ago.

"What is it?" I ask, pausing on my way to the door.

Forehead creased, eyes narrowed, he looks from his phone to me, then back at the screen.

The concern on his face has me heading to him.

I hold out my hand.

"Perhaps this can wait till you are back?" His voice tapers off, but he still doesn't hand it over.

"It can't be that bad," I say, a half smile on my face.

He doesn't reply. And that's enough to make me reach out and take the phone from him.

My heart stutters, before it slams into my chest and begins to thud so hard I hear the blood pumping in my ears.

My fingers tighten on the phone and I stare at the screen.

A YouTube video. It shows a boy approaching a girl. They begin to kiss. Passionate. The angle of the video such that it's clear they are equal participants.

No, no, no, it can't be.

My heart already knows even as my brain is registering and discarding what I see.

The boy steps back. They speak. This time the camera gives a clear view of her face.

It's me.

A much younger me, with a fringe. Hair curling at the end.

I watch her face the screen bare-breasted, her nipples clearly seen on camera. He takes off his T-shirt, steps close. They kiss again. His hand fixes on her breast. The video freezes, and we sit in silence for a few seconds.

"Sienna."

Eric puts his hand on my shoulder but I don't notice. My knees threaten to give out from under me.

Still clutching the phone, I walk to the large arm chairs by the window, sink into one.

Eric follows, sitting down in the other.

"That *is* you, isn't it?" He asks, voice hesitant.

I cringe, but don't say anything, my eyes still playing the images in my head.

"Fuck."

"Who did this?" He asks.

I force myself to meet his eyes, cheeks flushing at how he'd seen me in the video. No shirt, and in the throes of passion.

No judgment on his face. His eyes are clear. All I see is concern for me.

A breath I'd not been aware of holding rushes out.

I'm biting my nails again, but this time don't stop myself.

"Tom" I reply.

"Natalie's friend?"

I nod. Unable to sit still, I jump to my feet, and begin to pace back and forth.

"I can't believe that bastard released the video." I can't seem to stop swearing.

Then a thought strikes me, "How many people have already seen it?"

He holds out his hand and I hand over the phone to him.

"50,000 views and counting," He replies. "50,001. 50,020. 50,050."

He looks up, face pale.

It's rising exponentially.

"It was uploaded 10 minutes ago," Eric adds in response to my unspoken question.

"How did you find out?"

"Email," he says evenly.

Walking to my table, I place my handbag next to me. Hunkering down behind the computer screen, I scroll down my email inbox till I come to one from a name I don't recognize. A Larry Smith, and the subject simply says:

TED: This video will change your life.

Clever.

TED—Technology, Entertainment, Design—an organization known for inspirational videos. Exactly the kind of video everyone in Silicon Valley would open.

I am sure the email has gone out to everyone I know. *Everyone in my address book.*

"He hacked me," I say, voice bitter.

"Can he do that?" Eric frowns.

"No other explanation. The irony is that he's a lawyer. He knows how to cover himself. I'm sure he's hidden his tracks and I'll never be able to trace it to him. But he's the only one who has this video. Besides, he threatened me."

"He threatened you?" Eric walks up to me, leans his hip against the desk. "At the wedding? Did he know you were going to be there?"

"No, he came to attend Natalie's wedding. But when he saw me, found I was with Jace, he saw his chance. He was in debt, wanted money. I refused to pay."

I'm talking aloud more for my own benefit, so I can rationalize what happened here.

"I'd no idea he'd filmed it," I say.

We both look to the email with the frozen image of me on screen. I slam the laptop shut, then bury my head in my hands.

"It's not a big deal," I mutter.

I don't sound convincing, even to myself.

I've seen worse, of course. Sex videos are common; you'd never give it a second thought. *Except when you're featured in one of them.*

My phone pings a reminder. I need to leave now to arrive in time for the conference I was headed to.

I must go, and yet my body refuses to cooperate. I clench my fists, as my heart begins to beat at the thought of leaving this room. Everyone I know must have received this video. They'll know it was me. Worse, strangers will have seen it to. And now, I must face them.

"Want me to come with you?" Eric asks.

When I hesitate, he adds, "Moral support. That's all."

The breath whooshes out of me.

"No," I shake my head. "I need to face this. I was never one to run and hide."

"You are one of the most courageous persons I know." His voice is serious enough to focus my attention, take my mind off the video. "You were determined to make it on your own steam. And look at you." He gestures to the space around us, "You've arrived."

Yeah. I gesture to the video. "When you have a sex video on YouTube, you *really* have arrived."

He chuckles at that, and a reluctant smile tugs at my lips.

"At least I haven't lost my sense of humor."

"You're strong. You'd have to be to come this far." Leaning close Eric takes my hand in his.

I don't pull away. It feels wrong to do so. Not when he's been so understanding and patient.

His eyes shine with kindness, and hope. Warm, brown eyes. Nothing like the silver-green ones that rob me of breath.

"Eric." My reluctance gets through to him.

"So, no? I don't stand a chance, do I?"

Both of us look at the ring I'm still wearing.

Jace's ring.

Yeah, I can't bring myself to take it off.

I flush, can't trust myself to speak. If only I could love Eric, things would be so simple. Instead, I've lost my heart to a man with whom I don't have a future. One I'd left stranded in the worst way possible.

"I'm sorry."

Placing his hands on my shoulders, he kisses my forehead. "Don't be," he says. "Friends?"

I nod, hug him back.

He steps away from the desk, "Go now. Or you'll be late."

Picking up my bag once more, I walk to the door.

"I'll email YouTube and get the video removed." His voice follows me.

"Thanks, Eric."

His thoughtfulness only makes me feel worse. Why can't I fall in love with Eric? He'll be safe, secure.

Boring.

I can never resist bad boys. And Jace is as macho as they come. Besides, the chemistry with Jace ... I'll never have that with anyone else. Tears prick my eyes and I blink them away.

Turning, I leave, slamming the door behind me. Reaching the parking garage, I slide into the driver's seat. But I'm unable to start the car.

I'm not ready yet to face the world, not like this. Banging my fists on the steering wheel, I finally give vent to my anger.

40

Jace

Jace looks up from the last row of the conference room in the less fashionable part of Silicon Valley. The space is packed with hopefuls eager to make their pitch. A chance to get funding for their dream project is why so many are locked in this basement room that smells of coffee and take-out pizza. While a Frenchman in a sharp suit speaks from the makeshift platform.

"There's no shortage of enthusiasm and ideas in the Valley," he says. "Things have been frothy, and you see a lot of dumb money. But the music's going to stop and not a lot of people will have a chair." He crosses his arms, standing on the makeshift podium. His eyes swivel from one corner of the room to the other, making sure he makes enough eye contact to have everyone's attention. "There will be dead bodies. And blood."

The last word is drawn out. An exaggerated, sinister tone, which sends a titter through the audience of fifty start-ups.

Kids.

The average age of the crowd is twenty, or maybe twenty-five. Jace realizes he is the oldest in the room.

A man in the audience asks a question, drawing his attention back to the room.

Nowadays, most anyone with a half-baked idea seems to make a beeline to the Valley, pitching their ideas to investors, trying to raise their first $100,000 to get their start-up off the ground. Hungry kids, happy to sleep six to a two-bedroom apartment, all firm in the belief that it will be worth it in the end.

Little do they know what they are getting into.

Everyone talks about winning in the Valley. No one speaks about those who go from having everything to nothing. Like him.

After Sienna had left, Jace had turned up at Natalie's wedding. Darren had noticed Sienna's absence, of course.

Yet, Jace had waited till the next day, till the festivities had died down and Natalie had left for her honeymoon, before giving his father the news. He'd surprised Jace. He wasn't going to disinherit him. Not yet. He was giving Jace one last chance to redeem himself.

Six months more to find a woman and settle down.

Only, Jace knows the one woman he wants is never going to agree to marry him.

Ironically, the money that Sienna returned to his account had thrown him a lifeline. But even that hadn't been enough. Sienna's debts were miniscule compared to the billion he needed to save his sinking firm.

Jace had used the money to buy out Eric's share in the company. A deal completed by email—strictly business.

Now he has nothing.

Nothing except his ability to speak and convince. That is why he's here. To pitch his idea for a start-up.

On the proverbial other side of the table.

Jace curls his fingers into fists at his side, his muscles tensing. It had taken a lot of courage to turn up here. But he knows he must do it. It's time he surfaced and faced the real world. Put the mistakes he's made so far behind him, and move on. He'd been cocky, and proud, and sure that he'd succeed. He'd never even entertained the thought of things going wrong.

Never thought I'd fall for Sienna either.

Jace is not giving up, though.

He's always known his Silicon Valley sojourn was fraught with risks. Only he'd always known his inheritance was a fallback.

But not this time.

This time he's determined to make it under his own steam. Once he'd made up his mind about that, it'd almost been a relief. He hadn't realized how much his father's money had been holding him back, not till he'd made this decision to break free of it.

Perhaps Sienna leaving him had been a blessing in disguise. It'd given him the opportunity to re-evaluate what he'd become. Eric's leaving had hit him hard. He shouldn't have let his friend go.

He shouldn't have let Sienna leave either. He should have told her how he'd felt about her. He'd also not reached out to Karina and the guys since his return.

Me and my damned pride.

But Jace is determined to rebuild his business, find his future first.

He needed one pitch to go right.

Jace knows sometimes the difference between success and failure is a moment. A second and everything could change. All he has is hope.

The Frenchman has finished speaking, when the door at the back of the room bangs shut. The clap of heels is barely muffled by the fading carpet, as someone rushes up the room toward the podium.

Sienna mounts the steps up to the stage. Her pencil-skirt stretches across her flared hips. Slim thighs, a gently curved ankle.

"Sorry I'm late," she says.

Breath coming out in short gasps from her hurried walk to the podium. Her breasts, clad in the white shirt, move up and down, drawing attention to the skin of her throat sweeping up toward her oval face.

Strong jaw line. Stubborn. Distinctive.

It's her.

He'd been thinking of her not a second ago, and here she is.

Familiar eyes blaze a molten-amber as she walks onto the platform.

For a second, Jace is tempted to get up and leave. But he knows that will only call more attention to himself.

Besides, this is his last chance.

After being turned down by close to fifty—*fifty*—investors, this open pitch is all that lies between him and complete humiliation. If he doesn't get this money today, he'd have no choice but pack up and leave for London.

For good.

He'd have to admit defeat, go back to his father, beg for money. Even the thought of doing so stiffens his spine.

No, he's going to have to stay, and pitch.

To Sienna.

Even as he's thinking it, Jace risks looking up to catch another glimpse of her. Her hair shorter, cut differently so it frames her face, softening her jaw line.

He glances down at his jeans and hoodie. Over the past month of pounding pavement and pitching for investments, he'd realized it was best to play the part of the down-and-out of luck investor. It didn't help if he turned up for a meeting in a tailor-made suit reeking of old money.

Most people had met him more out of personal curiosity. For a chance to gloat over his downturn, to get back at whatever he'd snubbed them for in his better days.

The biggest snub he's sure is yet to come, when he pitches to Sienna.

And the irony of the situation hits him afresh. The change of sides is startling, as if it were all some cosmic joke. Not that he'd ever believed in fate or a higher power.

But sitting there, his ass already smarting from being cramped into the cheap bucket seat, his knees squashed into the tiny space in front, he wonders if someone up there isn't having the last laugh at him.

On stage, Sienna apologizes to the Frenchman, who kisses her on both cheeks before beckoning her to take her place.

He turns to the next team, asks them to pitch their idea.

Jace can't take his eyes off Sienna. She looks so different. Is it the grooming? The clothes? Or something more?

No, it's the confidence.

It's there in the tilt of her head, her spine straight, legs crossed showing those shapely feet in pencil-thin heels.

Seeing the turn of her ankle starts a slow burn inside him, and he clamps down on it.

The man next to him touches his arm, and he jumps.

Leaning in, the younger guy, dressed in a similar uniform of hoodie and jeans says, "Quite something, isn't she? A real hottie. She has guts too. You need to be damn strong to look the crowd in the eye, despite everything that's happened today."

His tone sparks of a feeling of possessiveness inside. A burning desire to punch the guy in the face has Jace curling his fists at his side.

No, he's not over Sienna. Not by a long shot.

If anything, seeing her after all this time only sends a pulse of heat racing through him. He's missed her more than he'd realized.

Then his brain registers what the man said.

"What do you mean? Guts?" Jace asks, still not taking his eyes off Sienna, who's now listening intently to the team pitching. Something about "tribespotting, meeting locals who share a passion for similar kinds of coffee".

The other man's voice turns suggestive.

"You mean you haven't seen the video?" The man chuckles.

"What video?" Jace doesn't bother lowering his voice.

For the first time, he notices the whispering in the room. The girl in the row in front of him titters, as if she's in on a joke. One he's not aware of.

A cold hand grips Jace's heart.

He turns to the other man. "Show me."

Phone whipped out, screen swiped to YouTube, and then Jace sees the video.

The sound of heavy breathing, then moans. Jace stares at the couple on screen. Lush auburn hair covers the woman's face. It flows over her chest, covering her breasts.

She raises her head, exposing the expanse of her throat. Then opens her eyes straight into the camera, a gasp leaving her lips.

It's Sienna.

A younger Sienna, with fuller features. Lips unpainted.

Jace knows the taste of those lips.

Sickness twists his gut. What the fuck is she doing in this video? *Who made the video?* And who is the boy with her?

Purple-black fury races through him, his fingers curl around the phone.

Another groan escapes her, and his body reacts to it, even as he curses himself. He tries to make out the face of the man behind her. It's pixelated but from his bony shoulders he too seems young, a teenager.

The camera freezes on her profile.

Who could do this to her?

More importantly, was she aware of being filmed?

She must know the video has been leaked.

And yet here she was, on stage, composed and facing the audience. No sign of worry or discomfort on her face.

Either she doesn't give a damn that people had seen the video or what they thought of her. Or she's doing a damn fine job of ignoring them.

In this room, at least, she had the power. And she was holding onto it. She was refusing to let the video get the better of her. That took guts alright.

As he's thinking that, she raises her eyes and meets his gaze, squarely. She freezes, her shoulders still. Even at this distance, he can see her go pale.

Sienna's as surprised to see him as he was to see her.

Grabbing her bag, she bends down to say something to the

Frenchman, kissing his cheek before leaving to walk out the side door.

The man next to him grabs his phone, pocketing it before jumping to his feet and joining the rest of his team who have been called in to pitch.

A low buzz breaks out among the audience, and Jace can feel most eyes in the audience following her out.

As he debates what to do next, the French man announces, "Ms. Murphy is not feeling well, but has asked us to continue with the pitch. We will share the results of today along with the recorded pitches with her and the final choice of five winners will receive $100,000 each. Investment from her will be communicated to all of you by the end of tomorrow. Now then—"

On his feet, Jace pushes his way between rows of seated people. Drawing more than a few irate comments along the way, he makes for the exit.

Adrenaline pours through his veins, as his heart thuds in his chest.

He can't let her go, not this time.

41

____

Sienna

I rush out of the conference room toward the parking garage. My heart's beating so fast I'm sure it's going to jump out of my chest.

Of all the places in the Valley, Jace turns up *here*. It'd been advertised that I was on the panel. Jace must have seen it, and known I'd be here today. Seeing him had cut through the sophisticated veneer I'd tried to project to the world despite the video circulating.

Walking through the crowded room toward the platform, I'd been aware of the eyes of the audience following me. The whispers, the stares. *Either they're talking about the video or my recent inheritance.*

Inside I'd cringed. The air, thick with unspoken questions, weighed down on me. Heart thumping, resisting the urge to bite my nails, I'd focused simply on making it to the stage.

I wasn't going to let the speculation get to me. I must stay strong.

My adoptive father would've been proud. He's always insisted I face every challenge life threw at me head on. That I never back down.

It's that iron will of his that had helped me make it through the early years of my new life in the US. When I'd wanted to fit in and had yet felt so out of place.

I'd felt every bit as out of place on that stage.

I hadn't wanted to come but the organizer had insisted, claiming my presence would help with the publicity. I'm now a minor celebrity. My inheritance story's all the rage in the Valley. The adoptee who inherited substantial money from her rich blood family and who'd decided to use it to help other starts-ups. Yeah, the media loves it.

They'd spun it as someone who wanted to share her good fortune by giving back to the Silicon Valley community. *The bankrupt entrepreneur turned Angel Investor.*

And then it strikes me.

That's why Tom released the video. The news of my inheritance was the last straw. Not only had I refused to help him with my then 'fiancé's' money, I had come into money of my own and still not helped him. And *that* must have made him mad.

This time, Tom hadn't even approached me for money, knowing full well I'd refuse him. Again.

Still, I hadn't expected him to release the video, had hoped our shared childhood years together would have made him hold back.

And now Jace has seen it, too. *Every man in that room has seen it.* No doubt they'd been thinking of fucking me even as I sat there on stage, face muscles rigid with the effort of not letting any of the emotions inside show on my face.

Now, my muscles sag with relief. I step out of the building and hurry toward my car. I reach for the door, when a shadow falls over the window. A hand covers mine. A shiver runs up my spine.

I know who it is even before I look up.

I'd expected Jace to follow me out. Would've been disappointed if he hadn't.

My eyes drink in the sight of him. Those silver-green eyes, high cheekbones, square jaw.

I'd missed him, had so wanted to see him.

But not like this. Not after he'd seen the video. Still, I can't pull away, don't want to let go of the feel of his hand on mine. My skin drinks in the feel of his palm, as it slides up my arm to my shoulder. Even through the sleeve of my suit, the warmth of his fingers bleeds through. Goose bumps spring to life across my forearm.

I turn around fast enough to take him by surprise. His jaw hardens as his eyes alight on my lips. It's like he's physically touched me. I shiver again. Pull myself together.

"What do you want?" I growl out.

Jace takes a step back. Lets me go to put up his palms and show he means no harm.

My eyes are drawn to his forearms, up toward the play of muscles across his shoulders. I realize then, what's bothering me.

He's dressed in a far more casual way than before. *I've never seen Jace wear a hoodie.* He's trying to blend in with the crowd inside.

No chance.

That familiar aura of power clings to him, one that will always set Jace apart from the crowd no matter where he is.

His face also looks thinner, cheekbones standing in relief to the rest of him. He's not been eating properly.

A surge of concern runs through me, and I clamp down on it. He means nothing to me. I have no reason to care for him.

When I meet his eyes, I flinch. Those silver-green eyes are exactly as I remember them. They stand out, even more vivid on his darker face. Right now, they're glowing with suppressed emotion, with pain and anger.

He's angry with me.

So mad that he can't trust himself to touch me for fear of breaking my bones.

I breathe in sharply, and pain twists my gut.

Why should I be surprised? I should not have expected anything different. Of course he's upset. I would be too if he had broken a promise and walked away at the crucial moment.

I put up my palms, my gesture meant to soothe.

The rage on his features fades away, leaving behind pain. And hurt. So much hurt. It vibrates off him. Lonely. He's so lonely. Confused. He feels betrayed. He'd trusted me, and I'd let him down.

"I'm sorry, Jace." The words burst out of me, and I'm not even sure anymore what I'm apologizing for. For him. For me. For what we could have been?

42

Sienna

The fluorescent light of the parking lot flickers, illuminating the blue-black of Jace's hair. Car brakes screech, then a vehicle passes by. It breaks the silence between us.

"Why, Sienna?" Jace's voice is stiff, controlled.

He's upset, accent more clipped than usual, his words like blocks of ice flung at me.

I shiver, fold my arms over my waist, hugging myself, to protect myself against his lack of emotion. That cold darkness he now exudes—dark hole that sucks away everything real and human about him, that is going to push him into doing things he'll regret later.

"I shouldn't have left you," I say, and his face goes still.

"You think?" he says, voice sharp enough to cut through me, tearing at pieces of me I thought I'd kept hidden from him, from the world.

I swallow at the leashed pain in his voice and nod. "I broke our agreement. I was wrong."

He stares, taken aback, as if he doesn't believe me.

Folding his arms over his chest, he leans back a little on his heels in a gesture that indicates he's waiting ... waiting for me to make the first move.

His jaw hardens. It's as if he's shut himself off, and I can't feel him anymore. And *that* disturbs me even more. It spurs me to take a step toward him. Then another, till our bodies almost touch.

He doesn't react.

But his eyes are fixed on my face. Snapped there with such intensity that the pale green glitters.

Heat spools off his body.

A flare of desire. I can't resist. Don't want to resist.

Rising to my feet, I brush my lips against his. Once.

No response.

Again.

Still, he doesn't move.

I slide my tongue over his lips, nibbling, trying to get him to open his mouth.

Still no change.

Then his muscles tense, lock into place, and a shudder runs through him. He groans, the sound torn out of him. I feel it rumble up his chest, feel it in that space where my skin touches his. It vibrates up his throat, but I don't let go. I deepen the kiss so I can swallow the sound as it rolls over his tongue.

He drags me to him, so suddenly my palm is caught between us. I feel him throb, feel the heat furnace off him in a dense cloud that pours over me, pooling between my legs.

I clutch at his shirt front as my knees buckle, and he yanks me closer, so close it feels like my skin is melting. He's all around me, and I can't breathe.

The pull toward him is so strong, I know I am precariously close to losing control. To him. Again. And I don't want to. Not this time. This time I want to set the pace. And I want to take my time about it.

I hadn't counted on things spiraling out of control between us like this. Meeting him unprepared has taken me by surprise. That on top of the events of the day. I must get away from here, from him, from how he's making me feel. My throat closes, pulse racing.

I push against him and he lets go. His eyes blaze, desire swirling in them, jumping off him so strongly that I almost lean back into him. My eyes drop to the front of his pants, his arousal so evident that a fresh flare of heat leaps to life in my belly.

No.

I take another step back till I feel the car behind me. His hands drop to his side. I know the moment his brain finally catches up with what his body is conveying to him.

Surprise slashes through the desire on his face. His eyes clear a little, but the green still wars with the silver. I can't look away. And I sense the struggle in him. He wants to close the gap between us, push me against the car, and take me right here. And I want it too. So bad.

"No."

I'm not aware of having spoken aloud. But he hears my refusal to the unspoken question.

Emotions twist across his face: confusion, anger and something else. Sadness. As if his insides are churning as much as mine.

Jace opens his mouth as if to speak, and then seems to think better of it. Then he runs his fingers through his hair, a familiar gesture that tugs at me.

"Not now," I add on a small gasp, trying to soften my voice. I grip my fingers together in front of me, so he doesn't see them shaking.

"What do you mean?" His voice is hoarse.

His hand goes to the front of his pants to adjust himself, and I redden.

"Needed extra space," he mutters.

I almost laugh aloud, shuffling my feet, trying not to cross my legs to cover the wetness inside. I don't want him to see how difficult this is for me.

He pushes his hands into his jeans pocket, looking uncertain.

A first.

I've seen him aroused before, but not like this, not sensing this deep want tearing him apart. And I know then I need to get out of here. Fast.

"You need money for your new venture," I say.

A statement, not a question.

He frowns, expression narrowing. A shutter falls over his face. Leaning back on his heels to put some more distance between us, he nods, the movement a quick jerk.

"I have the money," I say simply.

His gaze sharpens, turns almost predatory. He pauses, and then says, "It's no secret I need the funds, and fast. But why me? Why choose me over those inside?"

He laughs a little as if hearing his own words and unable to recognize himself in them.

It's obvious the turn of events is not lost on him. A month ago, I had no money. And now it's he who needs help. The Valley is a small place, like a village. And the gossip mills here function the same way. Only it also gets reported and spoken about in meeting rooms and in coffee shops, in the farmer's market and at Yoga classes.

Besides, everyone loves the story of a fallen angel, and that's what Jace is, after all. His story goes hand-in-hand with the one of my coming into sudden fortune.

Hell, if it wasn't true, if I hadn't been living this reality, I'd have refused to believe it myself.

I echo his words from our first meeting. "But I'm not going to hand the money over just like that."

I want to gloat but instead all I feel is weariness. A need to move past the anger between us. I'm also very turned on. I want to get my hands on him.

But I can't do it now.

Not yet.

"Oh?"

I nod. "Half a million dollars for sleeping with me. That's not so bad, now is it?"

He inhales sharply, "What is this? A power trip? You're getting back at me for trying to help you out earlier, Sen?"

Hearing him call me by my nickname makes me flinch. He's never called me that before and it affects me in a way I cannot explain to myself.

It also makes me want to lash out at him. "Thanks for your generosity," I say, my voice sharp. "I did return your money though, didn't I?"

He tilts his head, nods. "A gesture much appreciated. You helped me in my time of need, and for that I am grateful."

His voice is soft. And his response confuses me.

"Why aren't you more angry?" I ask. "I'd expected you to rage at me for having walked out like that. Perhaps even—?

"What? Seduce you?"

I redden at that. Yeah. Kind of.

I'd hoped we'd fight and then make up. Sweaty make-up sex with Jace sounds about amazing right now.

"You still don't get it, do you?" His voice is colorless, restrained. He wears an expression of disbelief, as if he's in on a secret I don't know.

I shake my head and slice the air with my hand. "It doesn't matter either way," I say. "I have the money you need. I can invest half a million dollars in your start-up, and once I see returns, the next half. On one condition."

His face loses color. He feels like a pale shadow of himself, going through the motions. As if the essence of him has withdrawn some-where deep inside.

I know the feeling well.

I can't understand why I'm putting him through this. I can't stop and yet I don't want to hurt him.

I love him.

The realization makes me gasp aloud. I slide my arms around my chest, hugging myself, wanting to hold this new knowledge to myself. I'm not yet ready to share it with him.

Taking a deep breath, I steady myself. Then say before I lose my nerve, "You spend the night with me, and you get the money."

"Are you kidding me?" He explodes. "Have you changed so much that you'd barter sex for money?" He grips my shoulders, gives me a little shake. "Money for sex? Is that what it comes down to, Sienna?"

I stay silent. Swallow down the words of protest that this is not me.

And yet this is also me.

I'm doing this so he realizes how it feels to take advantage of someone's helplessness, to strike a deal they have no choice but to accept.

But I am *not* going see it through to its logical conclusion.

Even though I feel compelled to get back at him for what he put me through, he'd helped me. And Jace had been a gentleman. He never did take advantage of me, not physically. Nor emotionally.

So I *am* going to invest in his start-up. In my own time.

"Four Seasons Hotel. Seven PM. Don't be late."

Turning, I get into my car, slamming the door, and drive way.

My eyes dart to the rearview mirror for a last look, but he's already gone.

43

Jace

After Sienna leaves, Jace spends hours driving around the city, till he finds himself at his usual haunt. The dive bar near The 99.

Walking into the bar, he asks for a whiskey, neat. It's not even noon. But he doesn't care.

Thoughts of being here last with the rest of the group, with Eric, fill his mind, a tug of guilt at not having called his friends since he got back. In the last month, he'd avoided their calls, emails, texts. Refused to even go to the gym.

And he felt guilty about having fought with Eric, and for letting him go. If he had a second chance, he'd handle it differently with Eric, perhaps explain his intentions toward Sienna more clearly. Hell, at the time he and Eric had fought, he hadn't been thinking straight. His feelings for Sienna had been so new.

But now... now he knows he wants her in his life. And he'd do anything to put things right with Eric too.

Downing half the contents of his glass, he looks into depths of the amber liquid, the color so like Sienna's eyes. Eyes that could look hurt, yet adamant at the same time. And always, always that powerful reaction he had to her, of wanting to immerse himself in her touch.

Her scent.

Her skin, soft yet supple, pulsing with a flavor that turned him on.

When he'd met her earlier, he'd sensed the change in her. She'd been more forward, more aggressive in a way she hadn't been before.

Even thinking of how she'd slanted her mouth over his had his gut leaping. She'd been so bold it had swept him away, engulfed him in a raging desire that had him wanting to throw her against the car and take her, right there.

And now, hours later, he's still aroused.

Finishing the whiskey, he asks for another. Swigs from the second glass.

He hadn't known she was going to be at the conference today. He'd heard about Sienna's coming into her inheritance, even as his father had turned his back on him.

Downing the rest of the whiskey, he asks for a refill.

Then, *that video*. If he could get his hands on the man who'd been all over her, he'd gladly beat him up for hurting her like this.

That the video was only of them making out, but not actually having sex was little consolation. He still wants to tear the eyes out of everyone who'd seen it. He wants to shield Sienna from the world.

He'd paid for his own mistakes, had no one to lean when his mother had killed herself.

But he could be there for Sienna, could show her he still cared for her, would be there no matter what.

She'd been shaken to see him too, and that gives him hope. It meant something that he affected her so much, didn't it? That's why he'd let her drive off earlier, had decided to accept her proposition, knowing this time he'd have to let her set the pace. Let her come to him.

That, and the fact that she'd still been wearing his ring.

He reaches for his third glass of whiskey only to have the glass snatched from his hand.

"Getting drunk in the middle of the day now, big boy?"

Karina.

He swivels around on the barstool, to find himself flanked by Damian and Arpad, Karina in the middle.

"Ah." Jace tries to speak. Find himself tongue-tied. His friends had been worried about him. He'd known that from their calls, emails, and messages. He hadn't thought they'd hunt him down here, like this, in the middle of the day. Just as the whiskey was beginning to numb some of the pain too.

He reaches for his drink, not meeting Karina's eyes. Perhaps something of his despair must have shown on his face, for she hands over the glass to him.

"What happened in London?" she asks, her voice quiet.

Jace downs the rest of the drink.

Arpad takes the empty glass from Jace, sets it aside.

"I fell in love," Jace says.

Karina claps her hands. "I knew it."

She holds out her hand to Damian who hands over a $100 bill.

"Jerry," Arpad calls out to the bartender. "Whiskey. Laphroaig, for everyone!"

Jace tells them the entire story, ending with how Sienna's waiting for him at the Four Seasons later this evening.

"And you are here getting drunk? Are you going to roll in smelling of stale booze and cigarette smoke?" Damian asks, his voice sad.

"I wasn't thinking," Jace replies.

"Of course you can't think straight, you're in love. Which is why you need us to tell you what to do." Arpad tells him.

"You didn't call us." Karina's voice is stern.

"I'm sorry." Jace swallows the guilt that twists his gut.

He reaches out, touches Karina's cheek, his gesture affectionate, before turning his eyes on Damian, then Arpad.

"I didn't want to worry you—ow!"

Jace looks stunned as Damian smacks him on the head. "Seriously? It's a lot worse trying to chase you down to figure out what the hell is happening."

"While all you did was sulk like a woman with a broken heart," Arpad adds.

"A *woman* with a broken heart?" Karina turns her gaze on Arpad, who meets it right back.

"A man with a broken heart too." He holds her gaze.

To Jace's surprise, Karina reddens, looks away without retorting.

"This is what you are going to do," Damian says, his voice stern. "Go home, shower. Wear your best casual. Nothing fancy. Comfortable yet fashionable clothes. Then you buy her the one thing you know she loves."

"Buy her what?" Jace asks, mind gone blank.

"What does she love? Flowers? Wine? Woo her, man." Damian slaps him on the back. "For a start-up investor from Silicon Valley, you sure have forgotten the basics of being a man. Of sharing what you truly feel. Have you tried telling her what you told us?"

"Tried telling her what?" Jace asks.

What is Damian alluding to?

Karina bursts out laughing. "That you love her!"

"Ah! Okay." Even as he says it, he knows they're right.

He'd never bothered to woo her. Treat her with the charm and respect she so deserves. Yeah, he's going to make up for it. He's going to make her feel special. Tell her how he feels.

He slips off the barstool, walks past them, heading to the exit.

"Jace," Karina says.

He turns.

"There's one more thing you need to do."

"What?"

"Eric," she says. "He's waiting outside."

Eric's here?

His friends have outdone themselves. They know all he needs is a chance to put things right between him and his friend and business partner. That he'll never forgive himself otherwise.

"You guys are all awesome." He flashes them a grin.

"We know." She blows him a kiss.
He turns and walks out.
Only to be hit by a punch to the jaw that takes him down.

44

Jace

"What the fuck—" Jace groans from where he's fallen on the sidewalk.

A hand grabs him, pulls him up. His vision clears enough for him to see it's Eric.

He touches the cut above his forehead, winces. "I deserve that."

Eric's fists, raised in front of him to attack again, hover midair, before dropping to the side. "Yeah, you do," he agrees.

"I was an asshole to you." Jace adds. "Was too caught up in my emotions, in what I was feeling for Sienna. I also felt guilty for what I'd done to us, Eric. For running the business into the ground."

Eric folds his arms over his chest, "You made some bad judgment calls. But that's how we learn. Chalk it up to experience," he says. "I won't apologize for being attracted to Sienna," Eric adds. "But I'm here to help you. I'm Sienna's business partner now."

"What?"

A familiar anger flares, then dies. "So, she chose to work with you?" Jace asks, his spirit sinking by the minute. "Are you two—?"

"Business partners," Eric confirms. "That's it. Nothing romantic between us. There couldn't be. Not when she only thinks of you. Sienna loves you. I've seen it in her eyes. Her reaction whenever you come up in conversation. Which is not *that* often, by the way," Eric clarifies, eyes twinkling with humor.

"She needs you now more than ever." Eric's voice turns serious, "When the entire world is scrutinizing her, judging her. She's putting up a brave front but she could do with a partner. Someone she'll allow herself to lean on."

Is Eric right? Can Jace get Sienna to trust him enough, to let him take care of her? Cherish her? Give her the space she needs to spread her wings and soar.

"You know about the video?" Jace asks. "Who could have done that to her?"

"Tom," Eric says.

"Tom? The guy from the wedding?" Jace explodes, "When I get my hands on him, I'm going to make him pay for this. Make sure he never dares come near Sienna again."

"I called YouTube, had the video taken down." Eric adds.

"Thanks, man." Jace holds out a hand, then changes his mind. "What the hell." Jace throws his arm around Eric's neck, hugs him. An awkward man hug.

"At least hug me properly." Eric swears. "Where I come from men don't hesitate to show their feelings for each other. It only makes you stronger to share what's inside. Know what I mean?" He throws his arms around Jace and lifts him off the ground.

When Eric releases him, Jace says, "You're right. It's what I need to do now. Show her the depth of my feelings."

"Go, she's waiting." Eric waves him on.

45

———————

Sienna

I'm waiting for Jace to arrive in a suite I've booked at the Four Seasons. I'd chosen the most expensive hotel in the city. To make a point.

I want to rub in how much our circumstances have flipped. That now I have the money. I hold the cards. *This round is mine.*

Yet, my emotions are all over the place, tying me up in knots. I think of him striding into this suite, and my mouth goes dry. Earlier, at the parking lot he'd come straight for me, those eyes burning me up. Those lips taut with desire, the slide of his hair roughened skin on mine. I curl my fingers into the palm of my hand.

Damn!

My thighs clench.

Already I'm aroused, so turned on. And he's not even in the room. *Not even here yet.*

The bell to the suite goes off, and I start. A shiver of anticipation runs down my back.

Still, I don't go.

I can't.

I'm rooted to the spot.

This is it. Open the door and there's no turning back.

Not till I've faced up to what I feel for him.

I know he wants me. And I want him too. It's the one thing I've been sure about since we first met.

It's what gives me the courage to finally move toward the door and fling it open.

And that's when he takes me by surprise.

He's freshly shaven, hair slicked back as if still wet from his shower. He has on an open-collared white shirt, over which he wears a khaki colored jacket with sleeves rolled up casually to his elbows, and a fresh pair of jeans fraying at the knees.

He looks calm, composed. Those silver-green eyes still, observant, but with a lingering warmth in them that makes me wary. As much as the bunch of flowers in his hand.

Lilies.

Starlight Lilies, distinctive large petals clustered over delicate filaments.

My favorite flowers. He remembered.

A wall around my heart cracks.

I take the bunch from him, inhaling their honeyed fragrance. Yeah, he's trying to be nice to me. Trying to get through to me.

He's succeeding.

I meet his gaze. A pleased look on his face says he knows he's surprised me. In a good way.

Then I notice the butterfly bandage above his forehead.

"It's nothing." He shrugs it off before I can ask. "Just went a few rounds with a friend."

"Does it hurt?" I ask, curling my fingers into my palm when I'd have reached out.

"And what if it does? Will you kiss it better?" he asks, voice serious.

The last time we had a similar conversation, also after he'd been in a fight—with Eric—it had led to us making love.

Liquid desire streaks through me as I remember that night.

He tilts his head. His lips curve, those sensuous lips that had brought me to the breaking point. He knows. Knows what I'm thinking.

I bite my lips trying to stop from smiling back in reply. Fail. My head is too full of the scent from the lilies to be angry.

"If I'd known flowers were all it takes to get you to smile, I'd have filled our suite with them." His voice is rough.

Silver-green sparks smolder.

His charm is once more lethal. I let it overpower me. Sink into that potent magnetism that is so uniquely Jace.

Nothing has changed.

Here I was, foolishly thinking I was in control, that I could play him at his own game. *I am playing with my own emotions.* My feelings for him. I had fallen for him, right from the moment I'd first walked into his penthouse in The 99.

Known already my life was going to change.

I'd resisted him then.

I don't want to resist him anymore.

The events of the last month, the death of my birth mother so soon after I'd found her again, has shown me how fragile life is.

Shown me that I, too, have limited time. That I want to fill my life with moments of beauty, of happiness.

Yeah, Jace made me happy.

Turning, I walk to the window, carefully place the flowers down on the small table. My view from this window is not dissimilar to the one from his apartment at The 99. Except he didn't live there anymore.

The Valley gossip blogs had been full of Jace, the fallen Angel Investor. How he'd broken up with his business partner, then moved out to a more affordable area, joining the 'normal' people.

Jace follows me inside, closes the door of the suite behind him. He walks into the room, stops halfway across the floor.

His stance is hesitant.

And that takes me by surprise.

My eyes swivel to his face. His eyes are clear, his face open. His features are relaxed. He, too, has been stripped of the walls he's put up to the world.

Without money, and with a company gone bust behind him, he feels more approachable. Vulnerable too... Sexy.

Yeah, it's very appealing to see him. See past his skin to the man inside for the first time.

There's also a determined glint to his eyes. He's hit bottom, tasted the bitterness of failure. But he hasn't given up. It's tempered him, made him even more determined to succeed. He'll overcome this setback. Make a new life.

Like me.

Even as I'm thinking this, he says softly, "I'm sorry. I shouldn't have said that. I didn't mean for it to come out like that. It's just..."

I open my mouth to speak but he stops me with, "Eric made sure the video is down."

It takes me a second to get my head away from that haze that always seems to envelop me when he's around. He means *that* video.

I redden, and my eyes slide away. I feel exposed, as if I've been caught doing something I shouldn't have. Yet the rational part of me insists it's not my fault. It isn't.

And then a thought strikes me. "You and Eric made up?"

"Yep." Jace nods. "Eric told me he's been helping you, that he's now your business partner.

"Eric and I, we—"

Jace shakes his head. "I know there's nothing between the two of you. I was an asshole earlier, that's all. Jealous and a little insecure that perhaps you'd prefer him to me."

"You're right," I say. "He's everything a girl would want. Strong, reliable, warm. Trustworthy."

"He is?" Jace frowns, eyebrows slashing down. Eyes haunted. Glowing with the beginnings of anger.

An expression I'm already familiar with. *So, endearing.* My heart twists.

"But he's not for me."

His eyes go stormy, the green swirling in a way that takes my breath away.

"You're beautiful," he says, and I flush.

"No I'm not." The words burst out. "I left you in the lurch. You lost your inheritance, because of me."

"I found *you*." His voice lowers even more. His words reach out to me, whisper over my skin. It's as if he's touched me across the space.

"Sienna."

I clear my throat, "What?" I ask. My voice comes out husky, aroused.

"You're doing it again."

I stare at him, uncomprehending. His eyes drop to my mouth and I realize I'm biting my nails.

I redden, and he chuckles.

The sound pushes right past the barriers I've put up over the years, touches that secret part of me. So, vulnerable, hidden so deep I've forgotten it ever existed. Until now.

The heat from his body surges over me.

For the first time, he too feels open. Really, open.

The last barrier around my heart falls.

A closeness, a connection, that feels so right.

We've seen life through each other's eyes, been through similar experiences, and this has only brought us closer.

When I move forward, he matches me, step for step.

Then I'm in his arms. His familiar scent, pine and cloves, surrounds me. He holds me close, placing his chin on my head.

A shudder runs through him. I grip him tight, pushing myself as close as possible to him.

Then his palm slides down my arm, sending a shiver down my spine. His fingers settle over mine, toying with the ring I wear.

The one I'll never take off again.

"I love you, Sienna," he says.

My heart stutters. Stops. Starts again.

Tears prick my eyes as he brings my fingers to his lips, kisses the ring.

"I'm sorry I left the way I did, that morning."

"Shh." He brings his finger to my lips. "You don't have to explain anything." That smoldering voice sends shivers down my spine. Will I ever be able to listen to it again and not be turned on?

My eyes lock with his. Silver-green temptation. I shudder as he traces the curve of my lips, then grip his wrist with my fingers, to stop him. "I want to tell you what happened. Why I had to leave that morning. I had a call from India, from my blood family."

After all these years, it's still difficult to accept that my blood family had tracked me down. That my mother never gave up hope of finding me. And she'd survived, waited, hung onto life till we met, till she got to know me again as a daughter.

I swallow the emotions that twist my heart.

His arms tighten around me. My soul mate holds me, as I tell him about going to Bombay. About my family, how my father had been killed while on duty. My mother dying in my arms. About Neil and how he'd taken care of my mother. Neil had loved her, I realize.

"He sounds like an amazing man. I'm glad you went, that you had a chance to meet your mother."

I lean my head against his chest and listen to the beat of his heart. Strong. Vital. Mine.

Turning my face up to his, I say, "I love you, Jace."

He bends, brushing his lips over mine. A touch. A sizzle. Filled with so much heart. Filled with... the essence that is him. Only him.

I feel safe with him. Protected. Safe enough to surrender to him. With him I am free. To be myself.

"Don't ever leave me again," he says.

"Never." I intend to keep my promise this time.

EPILOGUE

Four months later

When you lose everything, only to get it back a second time, you'll never take anything in life for granted again.

I fling open the window of the house Jace and I bought a week ago and lean out as far as I can, breathing in the crisp morning air. It's autumn, the colors across the valley reflecting amber and gold.

A dense wave of heat rolls over me and I sense him even before he slides his arm around me. Pulling me close, Jace places his hand protectively over my belly.

Bending, he lifts the hair away from my neck, rubbing his cheek against the delicate skin.

The familiar tug in my belly ... this time joined by a rolling sensation. Tiny waves travel out from my belly button, almost like little bubbles popping inside.

I stiffen, then whisper. "Did you feel that?"

When he grows still, I place my hand over his and we wait, both of us focused on that tiny space inside of me, where life sprouts anew.

Another flutter followed by a tiny punch and I gasp, caught by surprise. The life inside me knows us, wants to be part of our little circle.

I laugh this time, and then gasp when she kicks me as if warning me I only have a few months more before she joins us and takes over our life.

"We're still going ahead with the adoption, aren't we?" I ask, and sense him nod above me. We'd decided to adopt a child the very day I'd found out I was pregnant. I intend to adopt many more. Create a home filled with laughter and love, the way my adoptive parents had for me.

"If the Murphy's hadn't adopted me I'd never have come here, never have met you or had this life. I want to give back as much as I can," I say.

"And we will," Jace agrees. "And the app," he reminds me. "We need to get that baby launched before this one arrives."

"Yeah," I breathe out the sound.

Sheer joy grips me. I'm full inside, and not only with the child.

It's more, a lot more. A feeling of finding my space. With this person who is not perfect, but who has been through his own ups and downs and came out on the other side stronger. Deeper. More mature and more open.

That feeling of openness I had sensed when he'd walked into that room at the Four Seasons hotel has only grown since. It's as if once he started to give, he can't hold back.

Jace is making up for time lost, for everything he didn't have. For the feeling of belonging he so missed when he was a child.

Jace hadn't accepted my loan. He had plain refused to even consider it, until I had told him my idea of an app that I wanted his company to launch, and that I wanted us to be partners in it.

It's an app that will help match couples with adoption agencies. We'd also launched a grant. For couples who couldn't afford the adoption process, half the cost would be borne by our new company.

This would allow more children to find homes.

My parents would have wholly approved of it. Both sets of them.

After much urging, Jace had finally called Darren to tell him we were back together. And to announce the impending birth of our child. Darren had been overjoyed. He'd offered the next installment of his inheritance right then.

Jace had accepted, and funneled the money into a charity we'd set up. *Anja's Gift* now helps children in need around the world.

"You don't mind that my inheritance will not be there for our children?" He looks at me, the green flaring as I know it does when he's in the grip of intense emotion. Like now.

Jace is clear he intends to make it on his own, without his father's help, a decision that had earned him his father's respect. Now Darren calls us every week. Getting to know us, sharing the journey we are on in creating our own family.

"It helps so many more," I say. "You made the right choice." I pause to revel in our love, then speak again. "We're going to be late to meet your friends," I remind Jace.

I've already met Karina, Damian and Arpad. And Eric of course is part of our little family.

My mind skips across what needs to be done for the day, only to stutter, when Jace bites the side of my throat.

"They can wait," he growls.

WHAT HAPPENS WHEN A MAFIA KING HAS HIS PLANS SPOILED BY A SASSY LITTLE SPITFIRE WHO TAKES OVER HIS LIFE IN AN ARRANGED MARRIAGE GONE COMPLETELY WRONG. READ THIS DARK MAFIA BILLIONAIRE ROMANCE TO FIND OUT. CLICK **HERE**

READ AN EXCERPT FROM **M**AFIA **K**ING

Karma

"Morn came and went—and came, and brought no day..."
Tears prick the back of my eyes. Goddamn Byron. Crept up on me when I was at my weakest. Not that I was a poetry addict by any measure, but words were my jam. The one consolation I had that when everything else in the world was wrong I could turn to them, and they'd be there, friendly steady, waiting with open arms. And this particular poem had laced my blood, crawled into my gut when I'd first read it. Darkness had folded into myself like an insidious snake,

that raised its head when I least expected it. Like now, when I looked out on the still sleeping London city, from the grassy slope of Waterlow Park.

I could be the last person on this planet, alone, unsung, bound for the grave.

Ugh! Stop. Right there. I drag the back of my hand across my nose. Try it again, focus, get the words out, one after the other, like the steps of my sorry life.

"Morn came and went—and came, and brought no day..." My voice breaks. "Bloody, asinine, hell." I dig my fingers into the grass and grab a handful and fling it out. Again. From the top.

"Morn came and went—and came, and...."

"...brought no day."

I whip my head around. His profile fills my line of sight. Dark hair combed back by a ruthless hand that booked no measure.

My throat dries.

Hooked nose, thin upper lip, a fleshy lower lip, that hinted at hidden desires, Heat. Lust. Sensuous scrape of that whiskered jaw over my innermost places. Across my inner thigh, reaching toward that core of me that throbbed, clenched, melted to feel the stab of his tongue, the thrust of his hardness as he impaled me, took me, made me his.

"Of this their desolation; and all hearts
Were chill'd into a selfish prayer for light."
Sweat beads my palm, the hairs on my nape rise. "Who are you?"
He stares ahead, his lips move,
"Forests were set on fire—but hour by hour
They fell and faded—and the crackling trunks
Extinguish'd with a crash—and all was black."
I swallow, squeeze my thighs together. Moisture gathers in my core, how can I be wet by the mere cadence of this stranger's voice?

I spring up to my feet.

"Sit down."

His voice is unhurried, lazy even, his spine erect. The cut of his black jacket stretches across the width of his massive shoulders. His hair... I was mistaken there are strands of dark gold woven between the darkness that pours down to brush the nape of his neck. My fingers tingle. My scalp itches. I take in a breath and my lungs burn. This man, he's soaked all the oxygen in this open space, as if he owned it, the master of all he surveyed. The master of me. My death. My life. A shiver ladders away my spine. Get away, get away now while you still can.

I take a step back.

"I won't ask again."

Ask. Command. Force me to do as he wants. He'll have me on my back, bent over, on the side, over him, under him, he'll surround me, overwhelm me, pin me down with the force of his personality. His charisma, his larger than life essence that will crush everything else out of me and I... I'll love it.

"No."

"Yes."

A fact. A statement of intent, spoken aloud. So true. So real. Too real. Too much. Too fast. All my nightmares... my dreams come to life. Everything I've wanted is here in front of me. I'll die a thousand deaths before he'll be done with me... and then, will I be reborn? For him. For me. For myself. I live first and foremost to be the woman I was... am meant to be.

"You want to run?"

No.

No.

I nod my head

He turns his and all the breath leaves my lungs. Blue eyes, cerulean, dark like the morning skies, deep like the nighttime, hidden corners, secrets that I don't dare uncover. He'll destroy me, have my heart, and break it so casually.

My throat burns. A boiling sensation squeezes my chest.

"Go then, my beauty, fly. You have until I count to five. If I catch you, you are mine."

"If you don't?"

"Then I'll come after you, stalk your every living moment, possess your nightmares, and steal you away in the dead of midnight, and then..."

I draw in a shuddering breath, liquid heat drips from between my legs. "Then?" I whisper.

"Then, I'll ensure you'll never belong to anyone else, you'll never see the light of day again, for your every breath, your every waking second, your thoughts, your actions... and all your words, every single last one, will belong to me." He peels back his lips, and his teeth glint in the first rays of the morning light. "Only me." He straightens to his feet, and rises, and rises.

This man... he was massive. A beast. A monster who always gets his way. My guts churn. My toes curl. Something primeval inside me insists I hold my own. I cannot give in to him. Cannot let him win whatever this is. I need to stake my ground in some form. Say something. Anything. Show him you're not afraid of this.

"Why?" I tilt my head back, all the way back. "Why are you doing this?"

He tilts his head, his ears almost canine in the way they are silhouetted against his profile.

"Is it because you can? Is it a...a" I blink, "a debt of some kind?"

He stills.

"My father, this is about how he gave up on the mafia right? You're one of them?"

All expression is wiped clean of his face, and I know then I am right. My sorry shambles of a past... why does it always catch up with me? *You can run, but you can never hide.*

"Tic Toc, Beauty." He angles his body and his shoulders shut out the sight of the sun, the dawn skies, the horizon, the city in the distance, the rustle of the grass, the trees, the rustle of the leaves all of it fades, and leaves, me and him. Us. Run.

"Five." He jerks his chin. Straightens the cuffs of his sleeves.

My knees wobble.

"Four."

My heart hammers in my chest. I should go. Leave., but my feet are wedded to this earth. This piece of land where we first met. What am I but a speck in the larger scheme of things? To be hurt. To be forgotten. To be brought to the edge of climax and taken without an ounce of retribution. To be punished... by him.

"Three." He thrusts out his chest, widens his stance, every muscle in his body relaxed. "Two."

I swallow. The pulse beats at my temples. My blood thrums.

"One."

Michael

"Go."

She pivots and races down the slope. The skin of her dress streams behind her, scarlet in the blue morning. Her scent clings to my nose, then recedes. I reach forward, thrust out my chin, sniff the air, but there's only the green scent of dawn. She stumbles and I jump forward. Pause when she straightens. Wait. Wait. Give her a lead. Let her think she has almost escaped, that she's gotten the better of me... As if. I clench my fists at my sides, force myself to relax. Wait. Wait. She reaches the bottom of the incline, turns. I surge forward. One foot in front of the other, my heels dig into the grassy surface, mud flies up, clings to the edges of my £4000 Italian pants. Like I care? Plenty more where that came from. An entire walk in close full of tailor made clothes made to measure, to suit every occasion, with every possible accessory needed by a man in my position to impress... everything except the one thing that I had coveted from the time I had laid eyes on her. Sitting there on the grassy slope, unshed tears in her eyes, and reciting... Byron? For hell's sake. Of all the poet's in the world she had to choose the Lord of Darkness.

I huff. All a ploy. Clearly she knew I was sitting next to her... no, not possible. I had walked toward her and she hadn't stirred. Hadn't been aware, yeah I was that good. I'd been known to Lynch a man from ear to ear while he was awake and in his full senses. Alive one second, dead the next. That's how it was in my world. You wanted it, you took it. And I... I wanted her.

I increase my pace, eat up the distance between me and the girl...

that's all she was. A slip of a thing, a slim blur of motion. Beauty in hiding. A diamond waiting for me to get my hands on her, polish her, show her what it means to be... dead. She was dead. That's why I was here.

Her skirts flash behind her, exposing a creamy length of thigh. My groin hardens, my legs wobble. I lurch over a bump in the ground, the hell? I right myself, leap forward, inching closer, closer. She reaches a curve in the path, disappears out of sight. My heart hammers in my chest. I will not lose her, will not. Here, Beauty, come to Daddy. The wind whistles past my ears. I pump my legs, lengthen my strides, turn the corner. There's no one there, huh?

My heart hammers, the blood pounds at my wrists, my temples, adrenaline thrums my veins. I slow down, come to a stop. Scan the clearing.

The hairs on my forearms prickle. She's here. Not far, where? Where is she? I prowl across to the edge of the clearing, under the tree with its spreading branches. When I get my hands on you Beauty, I'll spread your legs like the pages of a poem. Dip into your honeyed sweetness, like a pen into quill, drag my aching shaft across that melting weeping entrance. My balls throb. My groin tightens. The crack of a branch above shivers across my stretched nerve endings. I swoop forward, hold out my arms. A blur of red, dark blonde hair, skirt swept up in a gust of breeze. She drops into my arms and I close my grasp around the trembling, squirming mass of precious humanity. I cradle har close to my chest, heart beating thud-thud-thud, overwhelming any other thought.

Mine. All mine. The hell is wrong with me? She wriggles her little body, and her curves slide across my forearms. My shoulders bunch, my fingers tingle. She kicks out with her legs and arches her back, her breasts thrust up, the nipples outlined against the fabric of her jogging vest. She'd dared come out dressed like that...? In that scrap of fabric that barely covered her luscious flesh?

"Let me go." She whips her head toward me, her hair flows around her shoulders, across her face, she blows it out of the way. "You monster, get away from me."

Anger drums at the back of my eyes, desire tugs at my groin. The scent of her is sheer torture, something that I had dreamed of in the wee hours of twilight when dusk turned into night. She's not real. Not the woman I think she is. She is my downfall. My sweet poison. The bitter medicine I must partake off to cure the ills that plague my company,

"Fine." I lower my arms, she tumbles to the floor, hits the ground butt first.

"How dare you." She huffs out a breath, her hair messily arranged across her face.

I shove my hands into the pockets of my fitted pants, knees slightly bent, legs apart. Tip my chin down and watch her as she sprawls at my feet.

"You... dropped me?" She makes a sound deep in her throat.

So damn adorable.

"Your wish is my command." I quirk my lips.

"You don't mean it."

"You're right." I lean my weight forward on the balls of my feet and she flinches. "What... what do you want?"

"You."

She pales. "You want to... to rob me? I have nothing of consequence, I'm not carrying anything... except." She reaches for her pocket.

"Don't." I growl.

"It's only my phone."

"So you say, hmm?"

"You can..." She swallows, "you can trust me."

I chuckle.

"I mean it's not like I can deck you with a phone or anything, right?"

I glare at her and she swallows. "Fine... you... you take it."

Interesting.

"Hands behind your neck."

She hesitates.

"Now."

She instantly folds her arms at the elbows, cradles the back of her head with her palms.

I lean down and every muscle in her body tenses. Good. She's wary. She should be. She should have been alert enough to have run as soon as she sensed my presence. But she hadn't. And I'd delayed what was meant to happen long enough.

I pull out the gun from my pocket hold it to her temple. "Goodbye Beauty."

WANT TO FIND OUT WHAT HAPPENS NEXT? READ MICHAEL BYRON AND KARMA'S STORY HERE.

CLAIM YOUR FREE PREQUEL TO THE SOVRANOS

CLAIM YOUR FREE PARANORMAL ROMANCE BOOK HERE

MORE BOOKS BY L. STEELE

FREE BOOKS

*CLAIM YOUR **FREE** PREQUEL TO THE SOVRANOS*
*CLAIM YOUR **FREE** PARANORMAL ROMANCE BOOK **HERE***
*MORE BOOKS BY **L. STEELE***
MORE BOOKS BY LAXMI

ABOUT THE AUTHOR

Hello 👋 I'm L. Steele. I love to take down alphaholes. I write romance stories with douche canoes who meet their match in sassy, curvy, spitfire women :) I also write dark sexy paranormal romance as NY Times bestseller Laxmi Hariharan.

Married to a man who cooks as well as he talks :) I live in London.

WANT A FREE PARANORMAL ROMANCE NOVEL FROM LAXMI, CLICK HERE

JOIN MY SECRET FACEBOOK READER GROUP; I AM DYING TO MEET YOU!

FOLLOW ME ON AMAZON

FOLLOW ME ON BOOKBUB

FOLLOW ON GOODREADS

FOLLOW ME ON FB

FOLLOW ME ON INSTAGRAM

HOW MANY OF MY BOOKS HAVE YOU READ? CLICK HERE TO FIND OUT...

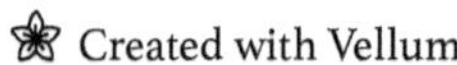 Created with Vellum

www.ingramcontent.com/pod-product-compliance
Lightning Source LLC
Chambersburg PA
CBHW071300190726
48292CB00007B/2616